Starscape Books by David Lubar

NOVELS

Flip
Hidden Talents
True Talents

SERIES

My Rotten Life: Nathan Abercrombie, Accidental Zombie, Book One
Dead Guy Spy: Nathan Abercrombie, Accidental Zombie, Book Two
Goop Soup: Nathan Abercrombie, Accidental Zombie, Book Three

STORY COLLECTIONS

The Battle of the Red Hot Pepper Weenies
and Other Warped and Creepy Tales

The Curse of the Campfire Weenies
and Other Warped and Creepy Tales

In the Land of the Lawn Weenies
and Other Warped and Creepy Tales

Invasion of the Road Weenies
and Other Warped and Creepy Tales

THE BIG STINK

Copyright © 2010 by David Lubar

Enter the Zombie excerpt copyright © 2010 by David Lubar

Reader's Guide copyright © 2010 by Tor Books

All rights reserved.

A Starscape Book
Published by Tom Doherty Associates, LLC
175 Fifth Avenue
New York, NY 10010

www.tor-forge.com

Design by Greg Collins

ISBN 978-0-7653-2343-9 (hardcover)
ISBN 978-0-7653-2510-5 (trade paperback)

First Edition: September 2010

Printed in August 2010 in the United States of America by RR Donnelley, Harrisonburg, Virginia

0 9 8 7 6 5 4 3 2 1

Nathan Abercrombie,
Accidental Zombie
BOOK FOUR

THE
BIG
STINK

David Lubar

STARSCAPE

A Tom Doherty Associates Book · New York

For John and Elaine Snyder,
Beth, Linda, and Michelle,
good neighbors and good friends,
even after they fled the valley

CONTENTS

INTRODUCTION

I figured, being dead, my life would become a lot simpler. I wouldn't have to take care of myself or worry about stuff like eating the right food. But dead kids have a whole different bundle of problems. I didn't lose my worries. I just swapped them for a messier set of problems.

1

Raising a Stink

"This stinks," Mookie said.

"It certainly rots," Abigail said.

I had to agree—it wasn't a good situation. But compared with being turned into a walking dead kid, it wasn't a big deal, so I tried to look on the bright side. "At least it's only for a week or two." I shifted around in the tiny seat. If I crossed my feet, I could barely fit my legs under the little desk. I almost felt like I was wearing it.

"Hey, you know what? We can pretend we're giants." Mookie grabbed his desk with one hand and lifted it up a couple inches. Then he growled and shook it.

"Cool. I hadn't thought of that." I stared at my desk

and pretended it was normal size and I was huge. That was fun. Down at the boardwalk in Wildwood, they have this giant chair. You can sit in it and get your picture taken. They have a giant pencil you can hold, too. It makes you look like a miniature person. I guess this was the opposite. The miniature desk and chair made me look like a giant.

"Well, fee fie yippee foe fum," Abigail said. "That makes it all better."

"I smell the blood of an Englishman." Mookie sniffed. "No, wait. My mistake. I smell last night's bean soup."

"Eww." Abigail slipped out of her seat, staggered away from Mookie, and sat at the empty desk on the other side of me. "Mookie, you need to register your digestive system with the government as a toxic-waste dump."

He patted his gut. "It's more like a national monument." He sniffed again. "Actually, I can't smell anything. I think I'm getting a cold. But you don't see me acting all grumpy."

"Yeah, what's up?" I asked Abigail. "You don't normally complain this much."

"This place brings back too many bad memories," she said. "I never thought I'd have to revisit them."

"It's all good memories for me," Mookie said. "Crayons, songs, puppets. Tons of good stuff. Especially the cupcakes. I remember lots of cupcakes." He smacked my shoulder. "Remember?"

I thought back. "Sure. With big globs of icing."

"Parents baked them every time someone had a birthday," Mookie said. "I had three birthdays one year because Mom won two hundred cupcakes in a radio contest and she wanted to get rid of them. I guess nobody kept track. Or they just loved cupcakes as much as I do. We don't have cupcakes nearly enough now. I miss this place."

I remembered those cupcakes. They were green. I think they were made with broccoli or zucchini or something. But almost anything tastes great if it has enough icing on it, so nobody complained.

Mookie stood up on his chair and shouted, "Hey, any birthdays coming up? Don't forget the cupcakes. You have to bring them. It's a rule here."

I guess I had good and bad memories, which kind of canceled each other out. Back then, the art teacher was always putting my stuff on the display board and telling me I had talent. I'd had a mean first-grade teacher who yelled at all the kids and smelled like mouthwash, but she quit, and the teacher who took over for her was really nice. So, unlike Abigail, I didn't mind being here again— except that everything was too small for us fifth-graders. Not only were the chairs and desks tiny, but the water fountains were so low, they looked like they were made for dogs.

"Hey, come on. Birthdays?" Mookie shouted. He

stepped up on the desk. I heard it groan, but it didn't break. "It doesn't have to be right now. It can be any time this month."

The bell rang and Ms. Otranto, our language arts and social studies teacher, walked into the room. She stared at Mookie.

"Sorry," he said as he climbed off his desk and sat back down. "I was taking a poll."

As Ms. Otranto walked toward the desk in front, which was full sized, she looked up at the drawings of nursery rhyme characters that lined the wall above the blackboard, sighed, and said pretty much the same thing I'd just said. "Don't worry, class. It's just for one or two weeks. We should be happy they had room for us. All the other fifth-graders have to double up and share classrooms."

So there we were, crammed into a first-grade classroom at Borloff Lower Elementary School while our own school—Belgosi Upper Elementary—got cleaned and disinfected. Apparently, the building had developed some sort of dangerous mold spore problem, thanks to the leak in the cafeteria ceiling. This had nothing to do with the giant slime mold I'd run into—actually, dived into—the other week. It was something that had happened to a lot of schools in the state. Either way, we were stuck here until the Board of Health said it was safe to go back to Belgosi.

Mold spores aren't good for kids to breathe. That's not a problem for me. I don't need to breathe. I could sit at the bottom of the ocean for a month without any problem. I could walk through a cloud of poison gas and not even blink. Mookie could turn every pot of bean soup in the whole universe into toxic gas bombs and I wouldn't care.

I'm sort of half-dead. I've been like that since my friend Abigail's mad-scientist uncle accidentally splashed me with a whole bunch of Hurt-Be-Gone. I don't feel pain. I don't need to sleep. I don't have a heartbeat, either.

As for being giants, I have to say Mookie nailed it with that description. Not only were the chairs and everything really small, but so were the Borloff kids. At Belgosi, we were already the big kids. Our school was for grades three through five. Being the fifth-graders, we were the biggest kids in the place.

Here at Borloff, we got to walk through the halls to our classroom with kids from kindergarten, first, and second grade. The kindergartners seemed especially small. I was almost afraid that I'd step on one, or that Mookie would trip over his laces, stumble into a group of them in the hallway, and crush them like bugs. Mookie trips a lot.

So we were the giants. Until the real giants shuffled into our classroom. Twenty of them. Big and scary. They didn't look happy.

2

Small World

The giants carried small chairs, which made them look even bigger. A man wearing a wrinkled green sportcoat and a stained red necktie walked in behind them. Even though he was a grown-up, and taller than most of the giants, he seemed kind of shrunken. He nodded at Ms. Otranto and said, "They found mold in the middle school. It appears we'll have to double up."

She turned toward us and said, "Pull your desks together as close as you can so Mr. McGavin's class can join us."

I jammed my desk against Mookie's, and Abigail scrunched closer to me. All of us pulled in and scooted forward. The big kids—I think they had to be eighth-graders—squeezed in around us and put their chairs down.

"Any of you have a birthday coming up?" Mookie asked them. "This is important. The right answer could mean cupcakes."

They ignored him.

Even after they sat, they were way taller than us. I felt like I'd been dropped into the middle of a redwood forest.

"Maybe we should read *Gulliver's Travels* to them," Ms. Otranto said to Mr. McGavin.

He laughed. "It would certainly seem appropriate."

The two teachers huddled together and continued talking. I glanced toward Abigail. "It's a book about a guy who visits giants and miniature people," she said. "It's actually an allegory."

"Thanks." I didn't need Internet access when Abigail was around. She could pretty much answer anything. Though, half the time, I didn't understand the answer. I guess I could have asked her what an allegory was, but I really didn't need to know. I was pretty sure it wouldn't be on our next test.

Ms. Otranto turned back to us and said, "What a wonderful opportunity this will be. Mr. McGavin and I have decided that we can create lessons that will be worthwhile for both our classes. We can all learn so much from each other."

I heard several snorts from the back of the room. "They're gonna learn pain," someone muttered.

Pain?

I glanced over my shoulder and found myself staring at the biggest kid in the group. He looked dangerously familiar, with the mindless eyes of a slug and the thick skull of some sort of tree-climbing ape.

"Who's that?" I whispered to Mookie. "He looks like Rodney."

Rodney Mullasco was the school bully. I didn't like the thought of him being crammed into a classroom with little kids. Right now, somewhere in Borloff, an extremely unlucky first- or second-grader was getting his ear flicked.

"Oh no . . . ," Mookie said. "That's got to be Ridley."

"Ridley?"

"Rodney's big brother. I've heard he's even meaner than Rodney."

"Oh, great." I wasn't sure my own ears could survive a flicking from that monster. His fingers were the size of jumbo hot dogs.

"What are you worried about?" Abigail asked. "You've tackled evil enemy spies and slime monsters."

I pointed over my shoulder. "None of them looked

this dangerous. And we're going to be stuck in here for all our classes. He can almost reach us from where he's sitting."

I turned back and stared at him. I can do that without getting noticed. Since I'm not really alive, people don't seem to sense that I'm staring. Of course, that works best when I'm behind them. It doesn't work very well at all when I'm looking right at them and they happen to glance in my direction.

Ridley caught my eye. I had to make a fast decision. If I looked away, he might decide I was scared, and he might also decide it would be fun to scare me even more. From what I'd seen, bullies like to pick a target for special attention. So it would be a bad idea to look away.

On the other hand, if I kept staring, he might think I was challenging him. That would be ridiculous, of course. He was almost big enough to put me in his pocket. But I had a feeling logical thinking wasn't his strong point. *Stare or look away?*

I didn't have to do either.

"Bee!" Abigail shrieked.

Everyone turned toward her as she leaped from her seat and swatted at the air. Kids near her ducked. I ducked, too, even though I didn't have to worry about pain anymore. I didn't want anyone to wonder why I wasn't scared. Ferdinand let out a scream and tried to squeeze under his desk. I noticed even Ridley had flinched. I guess eighth-graders weren't too big to be bothered by bees.

"Settle down, class," Ms. Otranto said. "The bee is more afraid of you than you are of it."

I'd bet she'd never been stung. I'd only been stung twice, but I still remembered how much it hurt. I turned around and faced forward. "I didn't know you were afraid of insects," I whispered to Abigail. I'd seen her lift a piece of rotting wood to study what was crawling around underneath it, or squat by a spiderweb while the spider was feeding.

"I'm not," she whispered back. "I'm afraid of seeing you get squashed by that monster. So I figured a distraction would be good."

"Thanks. It's usually Mookie who does something like that."

"He's too busy sniffling, sneezing, and begging for cupcakes. Besides, I don't think a gas cloud would have gotten Ridley's attention," Abigail said. "But he's definitely the type who would react to a panicked scream."

"I know what you mean." Bullies definitely had special radar for zooming in on fear. I hoped Ferdinand hadn't caught Ridley's attention when he dived under his desk.

Ms. Otranto and Mr. McGavin started our lesson. When it was time for math and science, our science teacher, Ms. Delambre, and the seventh-grade science teacher, Mr. Verne, came in.

After that, we got to go out for recess, just like at Belgosi. Except we had to share the school yard with the little kids and the big kids.

"Where should we go?" I saw there were already kids swarming over the swings and the other equipment. The big kids had snagged the ball field for kickball. Their version seemed to involve a lot of tackling, punching, pushing, and tripping. The little kids were playing hopscotch or tag.

We ended up sitting against the back of the building. That seemed to be the safest spot.

"Hmmm," I said as I watched kids running wild. "I don't see any teachers out here."

"I'll bet they all think someone else has playground duty," Abigail said. "With three schools crammed in here, there are going to be a lot of mix-ups."

"This makes me want to be real nice to the little kids," Mookie said as five enormous eighth-graders played catch with one of the smaller fourth-graders from our school.

"Yeah, I can really understand how they feel." I thought about BUM's mission. BUM was the group that was training me to be a spy. They'd told me about their goal when they first recruited me. *We protect people who can't protect themselves.* I was part of BUM. I had to protect that kid. I stood and started to walk across the playground.

Abigail caught up with me and grabbed my arm. "I know what you're thinking, but it isn't necessary. There are some mean kids out there, but most kids aren't like that. Most kids are pretty nice. Even the big kids. Look over there."

She was right. Four of the other big kids—two boys and two girls—were heading toward the bullies. They stopped the game. One girl even gave the fourth-grader a hug.

"I guess you just notice the mean ones more," I said.

"Especially when they're holding you up by your feet," Mookie said. He pointed across the playground, where Ridley was dangling Ferdinand over a puddle. "I hope he laced his sneakers real tight."

Lots of kids were watching, but nobody seemed willing to step up. "I gotta do something." I wasn't sure what. Maybe I could call in an air strike, or start a rock slide. Except we weren't anywhere near an air force base or a mountain of loose rocks.

"Wait," Abigail said.

"Nobody is going to stop him," I said. "It's up to me."

She tapped her watch. "Saved by the bell. Three, two, one, now!"

At that instant, the bell rang, and Ridley dropped Ferdinand.

"You set your watch to exactly match the school clock?" I asked.

"Doesn't everyone?" Abigail said.

"Probably not."

We headed in for lunch. They'd sliced up the periods so everyone could have a chance to sit and eat. Ours was the first of the three lunches, which meant the place was pretty clean. I didn't want to think what it would look like after the third group was finished. Probably like a trash pile.

"Some things never change," Mookie said as we reached the cafeteria.

He was right. It was just like the first day of fifth grade. "This stinks," I said.

"It definitely brings back bad memories," Abigail said.

3

Snot What I Wanted

Where **should we** sit?" I asked.

The popular kids had already grabbed the nice tables. We ended up in the back of the room, near a noisy vent fan. The table had one short leg and rocked every time anyone moved.

Denali shook the table, then held up the bun that came with her soup. "Rock and roll," she said.

"Hard as a rock." Mookie bounced his roll off his tray. He sniffled, then wiped his nose with the back of his hand.

Denali put her roll on top of her head. "Rock on!"

"Hey!" Adam slapped his forehead, then looked up at the ceiling.

A drop of water had splashed on his head. I looked up over him. There was a leak in the ceiling—just like back at Belgosi. It wasn't raining outside, but that didn't matter—the water came from somewhere in the pipes.

"This isn't fair. How come we always get the worst spot?" I pointed across the room at the sunny table by the window where Shawna and her friends were giggling and chatting. The way the light hit them, they looked like one of those old Dutch paintings you see in the museums. "We have just as much right as they do to sit where we want. Or them." I pointed at the jocks.

Another drop hit Adam on the head. "I guess this place will get closed next," he said.

"Yay—no school anywhere," Mookie said.

"We'll never be that lucky," Adam said. "They'll find somewhere to put us." He got up and went to the other side of the table. Another drop fell and splashed on the empty seat. "Hey, Nate, pass me my burger."

I handed Adam his burger. He opened his mouth to take a bite; then, just before chomping down, he stopped and sniffed. He removed the burger from between his teeth, held it closer to his nose, and sniffed again.

"What's wrong?" I asked.

"It smells funny," he said.

"It's cafeteria food," Denali said. "It's supposed to smell funny. They aren't allowed to sell anything that smells good. It's a state law."

"Not this funny." Adam thrust it under her nose. "Take a whiff."

Denali pulled back. "No way."

"How about you?" Adam asked Ferdinand. "Take a whiff." He held the burger out. Ferdinand screamed and dived under the table.

"Good thing it wasn't the chicken cutlet," Denali said. "That's really terrifying."

"Here." Adam turned toward Mookie. "You're the food expert. Is this bad?"

"I can't smell anything." Mookie pointed at his nose. "I got a cold."

"No kidding, Abigail said. "You've been sniffling and snorting like a bloodhound all morning."

"No, I haven't." It looked like Mookie was about to say more, but instead he wrinkled his nose, shut his eyes, and let out one monster of a sneeze. Right on the burger.

"Hey!" Adam yanked his hand back and stared at the burger, which now glistened like a large light-brown gem. Or maybe the eye of a fly would be a better description.

"Sorry." Mookie wiped his nose with his palm. "I guess I messed up your burger."

"It's yours now." Adam tossed the burger on Mookie's tray.

"Wow. Thanks." Mookie wiped his nose again, then grabbed a bag of barbecue potato chips. "Want these?"

"No. I want a gallon of bleach and a pot of boiling water. But I guess I'll have to settle for the slimy yellow soap in the boys' room." Adam got up and headed down the hall, holding his right hand away from his side.

Mookie wiped the bun with a napkin, then took a bite of the burger.

"Gross," Abigail said. "Someone sneezed on that."

"Not someone," Mookie said after he took a second bite. "Me. It's okay if I sneeze on my own burger. I already have all my germs. I'm not a stranger to myself."

"No, you're just stranger," Denali said.

Mookie sniffled. Then he held the burger up to his nose and sniffed. "Hmmm. I'm still pretty stuffy, but it does smell beefier than usual. But that's not a bad thing. Meat's supposed to smell beefy. Right?" He shrugged and kept eating.

Luckily, lunch ended soon after that, before Mookie could spray anybody else's food. Unluckily, we had gym next. Unlike lunch, it wasn't just for our grade.

We were doubled up with the eighth-graders. Worse, we were doubled up with our gym teacher and theirs. Worsest—and I know Abigail would tell me that's not a real word, but it's definitely the right one here—Mr. Lomux was back. He'd been out for a while, sort of thanks to me, and gym had been fun.

"Oh no," Mookie said when we got out to the field. He pointed at the middle school gym teacher. "He looks tougher than Mr. Lomux. Sort of like a bulldog."

Mookie was right. Mr. Scotus looked like a bulldog who hadn't gotten enough sleep. He was all muscles and bulges, with a snarl that could shatter a rock, and dark circles under his eyes.

"Hey," Mookie said. "Speaking of dogs, what kind of dog should a zombie get?"

"I don't know." I wasn't even going to bother trying to guess.

"A rottweiler," Mookie said. "Get it? *Rot*-weiler." He doubled over, laughing, until Mr. Lomux blew his whistle and told Mookie to stop fooling around.

We played touch football. Luckily, they didn't mix the classes together. We got to play with kids our age. "I'm glad we're not playing against Ridley," Mookie said.

I watched as Ridley stuck out his arm and clothes-lined two kids with one shot, putting them flat on their backs. I could just picture what would happen if he did that to me. My head would rip off and bounce across the field. A soccer game would break out as kids kicked my cranium back and forth.

"Ridley looks like he enjoys hurting people," I said.

"Just like Rodney." Mookie nodded his head toward the gym teachers, who were sitting on the bleachers, talking. "They don't care, do they?"

"It doesn't look like it." Another kid got taken off his feet when Ridley rammed into him with a killer block. He did a double flip before he landed. Ridley smiled like he'd just thrown his third strike in a row at a bowling alley. Rodney was doing damage, too, but I was on his team today, so I was fairly safe.

After gym, we went back to the classroom. It was crowded, but it was a lot safer than the field.

"You want to hang out?" I asked Mookie and Abigail after school.

"Can't," Abigail said. "Eye doctor."

"I can't either," Mookie said. "My mom won me these totally awesome sneakers in a contest. They're the kind that light up. We're going to get them right now."

I sighed.

"What's wrong?" Abigail said.

"It's Bear Season," I told her.

"Already?" Mookie asked. "It was Bear Season just a little while ago."

"Yeah," I said. "It happens twice a year."

"What are you guys talking about?" Abigail asked.

I explained it to her.

"That sounds adorable," she said.

"You're not even close." Hoping a giant hole would open up and swallow me, I headed home.

A Cute Discomfort

I **had the house** to myself for several hours, which meant I could totally relax and not worry about doing something that would make Mom suspect I wasn't a normal kid. But I knew it wouldn't last. When she burst through the door, her arms loaded with catalogs and posters, she was buzzing like she'd chugged thirty-two cups of coffee and a half a case of energy drinks.

The buzz had started as a small tremor a week or two ago, but kept growing as Bear Season approached. That's what Dad and I called it. Bear Season. It had nothing to do with hunting. That's when Stuffy Wuffy, the build-your-own-bear store where Mom worked, brought out its new line of bears and bear outfits. Much to my amazement, there were lots of people in this world who enjoyed dressing up stuffed bears in different outfits, so they looked like cowboys, kings, or clowns.

I guess it was good that Mom had a job she liked. The problem was, she liked it way too much and wanted everyone else to like it, too.

"Oh, wonderful—you're here," she said as she dumped her armload of goodies on the dining room table. "Don't move. I've got so much to show you. This is so exciting." She went back to the car for more. I thought about hiding, but I knew she'd just hunt me down.

"Come look," she said after her third trip. "We have all the posters and flyers. You'll be the first person in your class to see any of this."

And the only one.

I went over and let her show me a sickening amount of cuteness. Luckily, about ten minutes after the torture began, Dad walked through the door. Mom spun in his direction. I took advantage of the distraction and escaped into the living room.

Mom snagged Dad right away and showed off her treasures. I felt sort of sorry for him, but not sorry enough to stick around. I had the feeling she could repeat the demonstration to each person in the country, one at a time, and not get any less enthusiastic.

I flipped on the TV, plunked down on the couch, and switched to my favorite show.

Or tried to.

Instead of werewolves with flamethrowers, I found myself watching ice-skating ponies.

"What?" I looked at the little logo on the corner of the screen. It was the right channel and the right time, but it wasn't the right program.

I checked the guide. My program was gone. Just like that! I surfed around and found something to watch, but I wasn't happy that they'd killed my show. I felt like chucking the remote against the wall, but I knew that would mean I'd miss more than just one show. I'd miss television, freedom, allowance, and everything else that made life—I mean, death—worth living. So I settled for muttering a couple bad things about the people who ruin perfectly good TV schedules.

I slumped down on the couch. In the distance, I could hear Mom telling Dad all the stuff she'd already told me.

She came into the living room after she was done. I slid lower on the couch, trying to discover whether being dead gave me the power of invisibility.

Maybe it did. Mom walked past me. But then she stopped, walked back, bent over, and sniffed the top of my head. I wriggled away. She leaned over farther and sniffed my neck.

"Mom! Stop that!"

"Did you take a shower?" she asked.

"Yeah. Of course." I made sure to use the bathroom—both the toilet and shower—just as much as I had when I was alive, even though I never needed to use the toilet. It's amazing the kind of things moms keep track of.

"When?"

"Last night."

She frowned and sniffed again. "You need to scrub better." She walked away, but turned back and said, "And use soap."

"I do use soap!" What did she think—that I washed myself with sand? After she left, I lifted my arms and sniffed my pits. They were fine. No smell. I never smelled. The only kid in our class who smelled was Hubert Thuleau. He was also the only kid in our class who had a mustache. Or, at least, some whiskers on his lip.

Five minutes later, Dad walked past me. He stopped, too, and sniffed. Then he lifted his own arms and sniffed his pits.

"It's not me," he said. He went over and opened the window.

I was sure I didn't smell. Then another thought hit me: Maybe I was losing my sense of smell! My sense of taste was pretty numb, and I didn't feel pain. But so far, I could hear, see, and smell. It would be awful if I lost my sense of smell, or any of my other senses. But there was a very easy way to find out if my nose was working.

I went to the kitchen, opened the fridge, and took out one of Dad's cheeses. He likes this fancy stuff from the cheese shop over in Hurston Lakes. Mom leaves the house when he eats it, or makes him go out to the porch. I read the label. STINKING BISHOP. Talk about an honest name. I peeled off the paper that the cheese was wrapped in and took a whiff.

"Cheese!" I gasped as the rotting odor smacked around inside my head. My nose definitely worked— though it might be a while before it forgave me for sniffing something so stinky. Obviously, the bishop had died way before me, and then been kept in a warm, sunny spot, along with a bit of roadkill and a pinch of ground-up stinkbug. I put the cheese away and went back to the living room.

By the time Dad finished making dinner—in other words, by the time he'd pushed the right buttons on the microwave to turn the frozen family-size box of lasagna into a steaming-hot family-size box of lasagna—the Bear Season material had spread from the dining room through most of downstairs. The house was filled with catalogs and posters. Everywhere I went, I found myself face-to-face with a sickening amount of cuteness.

The whole time we were eating—or, in my case, pretending to eat—Mom talked about the new products. Right after she finished her last mouthful, she said, "And I haven't even started to tell you about the new wrapping paper and ribbons we're getting for the gift boxes."

"Jog?" I asked Dad as we started clearing the table.

He glanced over at Mom, who'd spent the last twenty minutes telling us about Angel Bear, who had a halo and wings; Diamond Gem Bear, who was covered with large jewels; and Tyke on a Trike Bear, who was the cutest cub ever—except maybe for Jammy Bear, who had adorable sleeping outfits complete with long sleeves, feet, and a hood.

"Jog," Dad said.

"Shouldn't you wait until you've had a chance to digest?" Mom asked.

"No!" Dad and I both shouted.

"That's a myth," I said.

"Exercise helps digestion," Dad added.

"Lasagna isn't heavy," I said.

We raced for our sneakers.

"It's just one more week," Dad said as we put some distance between ourselves and the house. "The stuff arrives in the store on Wednesday. Mom will be busy setting things up. By next Monday, when the sale starts, things will be back to normal."

"I'm not sure I'll make it," I said.

"Be strong. I know you think it's silly, but it's important to her. She's very involved in all of this. She actually helped design some of the costumes for the first time."

"Angel Bear," I muttered. I pictured Coffin Bear and even Zombie Bear. Where's Chain Saw Bear when you need him?

We jogged a mile longer than usual. That was fine with me. My muscles never get tired. And I don't breathe, so I can't get out of breath. Dad's in good shape, especially now that we jog all the time, so he was fine with the extra distance.

Eventually, though, we had to go back home and face the bears. As we turned the corner onto our block, I took a shot at asking Dad something that had been on my mind for a while.

"Can we get a game system?" If I had a game up in my room, it would be so much easier to get through the night. I don't sleep, so I'm always looking for things to do. I spent a lot of time on the computer, but I had to sneak downstairs and be real quiet. That took a lot of the fun away.

"We?" he asked.

"There are all sorts of cool games for grown-ups," I said.

"This grown-up doesn't have time for games," he said.

I realized I was using the wrong approach. "Can I get a game system?"

"What do they cost?" Dad asked.

"Three or four hundred for a really good one." As I said the numbers, I realized how large they sounded. "Maybe a little less."

"Plus money for games, right?" Dad asked. "And controllers, and all the other things you can hook up to a system."

"I guess."

"Well, we can't afford that right now. I just got the car fixed, and it cost a lot more than I'd expected. But if you save up, you have my permission to buy a system, and I'll treat for the first game. That's the best I can do right now."

"Thanks." I guess it was better than nothing. Though I was nowhere close to having that kind of money saved up.

When we got inside, I excused myself to check my e-mail. I was surprised by what I found.

5

Sic Transit

I had the usual e-mails waiting for me. Abigail sent me a link to a funny picture with a cat. Mookie sent me a link to some stupid jokes and a video of a guy getting smacked in the head with a frozen salmon. Nothing surprising there. But then there was this one:

From: PeterPlowshare@freemailer.com
To: Nathan316@tepidmail.com
Meet me on the other side of the elevators.

I didn't have to be a superspy to decode the message. Peter Plowshare was the name Mr. Murphy used in the online role-playing game where he first got in touch with me. "The elevators" could be only one place. Mr. Murphy wanted me to meet him tonight at BUM headquarters. I got there by taking an elevator from the Museum of Tile and Grout. All of BUM's elevators seemed to be hidden in places where nobody would want to go. That was pretty clever of them.

I was amazed he'd used e-mail. He was always contacting me in the weirdest ways, using stuff like robot bats or laser beams. He was really big on secrecy. I guess that made sense, since he was a spy. Then again, I was a spy, too. Even so, I didn't think there was anything wrong with sending messages the normal way.

I was just glad to hear from him. He'd gotten roughed up pretty badly by the evil guys from RABID. He didn't talk about what they'd done, but I was pretty sure it wasn't nice.

After my parents went to bed, I slipped out of the house and went to the museum. The door was unlocked, and a lady was sitting at the desk inside. I went in and took the elevator. It wasn't like any other elevator I'd ever been in. It was more like a roller coaster, or a rocket ship. After I pulled down the lap bar, the car shot toward BUM headquarters. I didn't even know where that was.

"Mission?" I asked Mr. Murphy when I got out of the elevator. I was eager for another assignment. My last one had been pretty dangerous, but it was also exciting. It was like I'd been tossed inside a video game.

"Soon," he said. "Right now, we have lots more training and field tests. You're still wet behind the ears."

I reached up and felt behind my ear, then held up my finger. "No, I'm not. See?"

"It's just an expression. It means you're still very new at this. You have a lot to learn. That's why I called you here tonight."

"You sent me an e-mail," I said. "I thought you didn't do that."

He shrugged. "I figured I'd give in to your constant nagging and try it your way. But don't think you can start making suggestions about everything. As I already mentioned, you're still not much more than an infant when it comes to spycraft." He pointed to one of the other elevator doors that lined the wall. "Let's head out. This is going to be interesting."

We took another ride. I went first and waited for Mr. Murphy on the other side. From what I'd seen, some of the elevators had double seats, but most had only one.

I found myself in the lobby of the Tor Johnson Fan Club National Headquarters.

"Who's Tor Johnson?" I asked Mr. Murphy.

"No idea." He led me out to the street. There was an empty car at the curb. We got in and Mr. Murphy drove us down the street, following directions from the GPS. After we'd gone a mile or two, he pulled over near a driveway with fancy brick columns on either side. The driveway stretched up the hill and out of sight between two rows of large trees.

"Here we are." He got out.

I didn't bother asking him what we'd be doing. He never told me anything unless he felt I needed to know. He didn't seem to understand curiosity.

Halfway up the driveway, at the top of the hill, we reached a stone wall with a metal gate. Past the bars of the gate, at least another hundred yards away, I saw a mansion. It was three stories high, and nearly as big as the middle school.

"Cool. Are we meeting someone there?" I wondered whether there'd be a butler.

"Not quite." Mr. Murphy unlocked the gate on the wall and swung it out. I noticed he'd used his lock picks.

When he caught me staring, he said, "It's always good to keep in practice."

As we started to walk through the opening, his knee buckled and he grabbed the gate to keep from dropping to the ground. He let out a groan and gritted his teeth.

"You okay?" I guess he was still hurting from his time with the bad guys.

"I'm fine, lad. No need to be concerned. Go ahead.

I'll meet you by that oak tree in a minute." He leaned over and rubbed his knee.

I headed toward the tree, which was about twenty yards from the house. Just before I reached it, I saw something racing toward me from the side of the house.

Guard dogs.

Three of them. They were dark streaks against the lawn, shooting toward me like homing missiles.

They didn't bark. But I could hear low growls.

I saw another motion out of the corner of my eye and then heard a clank. Mr. Murphy has gone back outside the wall and closed the gate.

My brain told me to run. I almost listened to it. But then I remembered the first time I'd met a stray dog. I was in town with Dad. I couldn't have been more than four or five. The dog was wagging its tail, but when it got close, it growled. I turned away. Dad put a hand on my shoulder.

"Don't run," he'd told me.

I said I was scared.

"I know," he said. "There's nothing wrong with that. But dogs chase you if you run. It's instinct."

I'd stayed still. The dog sniffed my leg, then turned and ran off. Dad had stood right next to me the whole time. I knew he'd never let me get hurt.

Of course, that hadn't been a guard dog. Or three of them. Either way, unless I thought I could reach the gate before the dogs reached me, it would be a bad idea to run. I was a good runner, but I was pretty sure the dogs would be faster.

By the time I thought through all of this, the dogs had reached me. They raced up to me like they were eager to start tearing me apart in three different directions. Maybe it had been a mistake not to run.

6

Pass the Salt

I wondered whether there'd be enough of me left to glue together when they were done. I didn't even want to think about how much it would hurt. When I glue a finger back on, I have this huge flash of pain. It doesn't last long, but it hurts more than anything I'd felt when I was alive. Gluing all of me back together would be unimaginably horrible.

But all three of the dogs did the strangest thing. If dogs could shrug, that's what I'd say they did. They just totally lost interest in me—like someone had flipped a switch and I'd turned invisible.

For an instant, I wondered whether Mr. Murphy was

pointing some sort of invisibility ray at me. I held up a hand. I could see myself. And nothing had blown up yet. So I knew I wasn't dealing with BUM inventions. They tended to explode.

I took a slow backward step toward the gate. The dogs, who were trotting to the house, didn't even look back. I took another step. No problem.

When I reached the wall, Mr. Murphy pulled the gate open for me. "Excellent. Dr. Cushing predicted this."

I glanced over my shoulder at the mansion. "What are you talking about?"

"She was pretty sure that domesticated animals, including trained guard dogs, wouldn't view you as a living creature. This is splendid. It opens up all sorts of possibilities."

"But this wasn't her idea, was it?" I knew Dr. Cushing would never expose me to danger. She really seemed to care about me.

"No. I'm proud to say, I thought up the perfect test myself." Mr. Murphy walked down the driveway.

I noticed he wasn't limping. "Wait. You were faking with your knee?"

"I couldn't very well walk in there with you, could I? We needed to see how the dogs reacted to you by yourself. And I certainly had no desire to be torn to pieces. I'm glad you found my pain so convincing. In my youth, I actually did consider a career in the theater. I suspect I would have been quite good."

I was going to shout at him for tricking me, but the scary thing was that, by now, I was sort of used to him doing stuff like this to me. It wasn't even close to the worst stunt he'd pulled.

As we walked away, I asked, "So whose house is this?" I was sorry I didn't get a chance to go inside. I had a feeling it would have been awesome.

"No idea," he said. "We just tracked down the nearest place with guard dogs. It's not like we'd keep dogs around just in case a dead kid like you showed up."

"No. That would be silly." Of course, half the things BUM did seemed silly. But the other half helped save a lot of people. So I guess I could put up with some silliness. "Are we doing anything else tonight?"

"No," Mr. Murphy said. "That's enough for now."

We headed back to BUM. When we got there, Mr. Murphy handed me a book. "You might enjoy this."

I looked at the title: *Great Spies: Their Secret Stories.* "That looks good."

"The more we know about the past, the better we can shape the future," he said. "That's why we study history."

He sounded like Ms. Otranto. But that wasn't a bad thing.

I went home from there. I still had a lot of time to

kill. So I started reading the book. It was pretty cool. There were all sorts of spies. Some just did one mission. Others spied for years. Some got caught and suffered terrible punishments. The ones I read about had helped our country in all sorts of ways. It felt nice to be part of that, even if almost nobody knew what I'd done.

I finished half the book by sunrise. I heard Dad drive off early, like he did most mornings. Then I heard Mom go. That was unusual. She liked to be here when I headed out for school. But it was Bear Season, so I guess she was excited about going to Stuffy Wuffy and getting ready to set up all those shelves full of cuteness.

She'd left me a note and a box of cereal. That was good. If she wasn't around, I didn't have to pretend to eat. Since I don't digest anything I swallow, it's a good idea for me not to put food in my stomach. Whatever I ate would just stay down there and rot. As I'd learned the hard way, the results could be pretty unpleasant.

She'd also left me a brand-new Stuffy Wuffy cereal bowl. It's a good thing I didn't have any appetite to kill. I put a few flakes of cereal and a splash of milk in the bowl and left it in the sink.

After my non-breakfast, I headed out to school. As I walked past the neighbor's house, Spanky, their dalmatian, ran over to me. He stopped right in front of me, panting and looking up. I couldn't help thinking about the guard dogs. Unlike them, Spanky was about as dangerous as a stuffed teddy bear. Or an unstuffed one, for that matter.

"Hi, boy." I reached out to pet him.

He sniffed my hand, then started licking my fingers like they'd been smeared with peanut butter.

"Quit it!"

Spanky kept licking. I pulled my hand away. He whined like I'd stolen his food bowl.

"I have to go." I headed down the street. Spanky followed after me, sniffing at my hand.

I stopped and turned around. "Go home, boy."

He cocked his head like he couldn't believe I didn't want to hang out with him.

"Home. Now."

He gave my hand another lick. I remembered how he'd almost run away with my thumb after I broke it off.

"No!" I yanked my hand away. "Bad dog! Go!"

He left. But he looked so sad, with his head slunk down and his tail drooping, I felt bad about shouting at him.

When I got to school, Mookie came running up to me, waving a comic book. Abigail was behind him, shaking her head slowly.

I noticed something flashing. He was wearing sneakers with lights. But they didn't have tiny little LEDs.

They had a small lightbulb—like the kind in a fridge—screwed into each toe.

"Are those your new sneakers?" I asked.

"Yeah. Cool, huh?" Mookie said.

"And they were free?" From what I'd seen, Mookie's mom never won anything that was really free, or really worth winning.

"Yeah. Totally. Except we had to buy the bulbs. They gave us an awesome deal on a case of them. I've got enough bulbs now to last me for years. But that's not important. I have something even better to tell you about. I figured out the answer yesterday."

I waited for him to continue, but he got a strange look on his face, opened his mouth wide, and let out a monster burp.

"That's the answer?" I asked. "I hate to think what the question was."

"Sorry. My stomach has been weird ever since I ate that burger. I only had two helpings of pork chops at dinner last night. But forget that. This is so cool. I realized it was crazy hoping I could find a cure for you by watching movies."

"I'm glad you finally figured that out," I said. Mookie had watched every zombie move he could find, hoping to find some clue about how to bring me back to life. "Though I have to admit, the movies helped us figure out how to find the bad guys from RABID when we needed to."

Mookie nodded. "Yeah. But they still aren't going to make you alive again."

"For sure."

"That's why I switched to a much better source of information." Mookie held up an old comic book. "This has all the answers. I found it at the used-book store. You know, the one where the guy yells at you if you don't buy something."

I looked at the cover. *Evil Zombie Rebellion.* The picture was pretty gory, even for a comic book. Apparently, when evil zombies rebel, body parts go flying. "That's gonna help?"

"Yup. I can't believe how simple it is. The book says you can be cured if I give you salt to eat. Check it out." Mookie flipped to a page near the end of the comic.

"Let me see." I took the book and read the panels.

The first panel showed zombies running wild through a town. The next showed a lab in a college. In the last panel on the page, a creepy old professor was talking to a young professor. In the balloon over his head, it read: "*If a zombie is fed salt, he will instantly come out of his spell.*"

"See?" Mookie said. "It happens instantly. We can cure you right away. How great is that?"

I had a feeling it wouldn't be that simple. I turned

the page. In the next panel, the old professor was still talking. *"The revived zombie will then turn on his creator and kill him."*

I pointed out that part to Mookie. "Did you happen to notice this little detail?"

He frowned, leaned closer, and looked at the page. "Oh. I got so excited when I read about the salt that I didn't bother reading the rest." He sighed. His head flopped forward until his chin pressed against his chest. But then his head shot up and he said, "Hey—that's not a problem. Your creator is Abigail's uncle Zardo. And he's nowhere near here. So you don't have to worry about hurting him."

"Look, it doesn't matter where he is. The problem is that this is just a story. It won't help me."

"We won't know until we try," Mookie said. "Let's get some salt." He raced off.

"This is crazy, right?" I asked Abigail.

"Yeah. Even if it happened to be true, which it isn't, that's all about the classic type of zombie. That's the problem. There are at least three kinds of zombies."

"Three?" I asked.

"Sure. First you have the ones from the myths and legends from the Caribbean Islands. Then the movies came along and did all that brain-eating stuff, which they totally made up. And now there's the third kind."

"Me?" I guessed.

She nodded. "You. You're one of a kind."

Mookie came running back, holding a packet of salt, like the kind you get with fast food. "I snuck into the teacher's lunchroom," he said. "Man, they have some weird signs on the walls. Who knew people were so worried about someone not washing a coffee cup?"

He tore the top off the packet. "Stick out your tongue."

I didn't bother arguing. I stuck out my tongue. Mookie poured out the salt. Then he jumped back.

"What are you doing?" Abigail asked.

"I don't want him to kill me by mistake," Mookie said. "He might not be totally in control when he comes out of his trance."

"Nathan isn't in a trance," Abigail said, "and he's certainly not killing anyone."

She was right about that. The salt wasn't even dissolving. It just sat on my tongue. Without thinking, I swallowed it. Then I jerked my arms, let out a growl, and spun toward Mookie.

7

Dare I Wear a Peach?

Brains!" **I** **shouted**, lurching at Mookie.

"Yeek!" He stumbled back, fell on his butt, and let out another monster burp.

I staggered forward. "Must kill my maker!"

Mookie scooted back like a dog scratching itself on a carpet. "I don't have any brains! Ask anyone."

"Maker must die." I took one more step, then started laughing.

Mookie stared at me for a moment. "Okay, I get it. You're joking. Right?"

"Well, after all those zombie jokes you make, can you blame me?"

"I guess not. That was a pretty good one. You really fooled me." He got up and rubbed his stomach. "I almost lost my lunch."

"Sorry."

He glanced down and said, "I think I might need to change my pants."

"Ick," Abigail said.

Mookie reached down the back of his pants like Dilby the Digger, except he used only one hand. He felt around for a second, then said, "Nope. I'm okay."

"That's good." I didn't want to scare him *that* badly.

"I'm glad you're not going to kill anyone," Mookie said. "But I wish the cure worked."

"Me, too. Thanks for doing all that research." I guess it was nice he was trying to help me. And even though I knew it wouldn't bring me back to life, that didn't mean there wasn't a small part of me that believed it might work.

"Don't give up," Mookie said. "I got a whole stack of comics to go through. I'll find the cure."

We headed to our classroom. Ms. Otranto and Mr. McGavin had cooked up a lesson for us about the worst kings and emperors of all time. It was actually pretty interesting. Especially when the people decided to get rid of a ruler.

I tried not to look back at Ridley. So far, I'd managed

to avoid attracting his attention again. Ferdinand was out sick today. Probably recovering from being dropped into a puddle. So Ridley needed another victim he could torture until he crumpled. The problem was, I wasn't a crumpler anymore. Even if I didn't have a chance, I knew I'd stand up for myself. But it looked like it wasn't going to be a problem for long. On the news last night, they said our school would be open again by a week from Wednesday.

After the lesson, we headed out for recess. Mookie, Abigail, and I sat against the building again and watched the other kids. After a while, I looked at my hand and sighed.

"What's wrong?" Abigail asked.

I rubbed my fingers against my palm. "My skin's all dry and flaky."

"No problem," Abigail said. "I have this great hand lotion." She opened her purse and pulled out a bottle filled with some light-pink gunk. It looked like liquid bubble gum.

"No way," I said. For a girl genius, she sure carried around a lot of silly stuff.

"Come on. Try it." She flipped the lid and held the bottle out. "It has emollients. Trust me. I guarantee it will make your skin feel better."

"Okay, but just a little." I opened my hand and let her

squirt some of the gook into it. Then I rubbed my hands together. "Not bad," I said. My skin did seem a bit better.

"And you smell nice," Mookie said.

"What?"

"Peach," Abigail said.

"Oh, great." I sniffed my hands. It was like I'd jammed my nose deep into a fruit bowl. "I can't go through the rest of the day smelling like a peach."

"I don't think you have much choice," Abigail said.

"Not to mention, the rest of my life."

"You won't have to," Abigail said. "There are all sorts of aromas. Strawberry, vanilla, and a variety of flowers. Violets are great. So is lilac. It's very soothing."

I let her go on. There didn't seem to be any way to stop her. When she was finished, I asked her, "Do they make any kind of hand lotion that doesn't smell?"

"Sure," Abigail said. "But what fun would that be?"

The bell rang. Ridley was standing right in front of the door. Two of his friends were there with him. They were watching our class as we walked inside.

"Guess they're looking for a victim," Mookie said. "They're going to pick me. I know it."

"Well, you are kind of easy to notice." I pointed to his sneakers.

"Oh, no." Mookie bent over and loosened both bulbs so they stopped flashing.

"This is a good time to be invisible," Abigail said. "Just keep walking and don't look at them."

"Sounds like a smart plan," I said. It would be easy enough for me. I had all of that spy training. I could slip past people like a shadow.

You don't see me, I thought as I walked past Ridley. I was a spy. I was a ninja. I was a Jedi. I was invisible.

Ridley put his hand on my shoulder. "Hey, kid, you smell like a peach."

I froze and looked up at him. The best answer seemed to be the simplest one. "Yeah. I do."

He shoved me. "I don't like peaches."

"Sorry to hear that." I moved back a step.

"In fact, I *hate* peaches." Ridley curled his hands into fists. This wasn't good. I could tell he was just looking for an excuse to hurt me. Actually, he couldn't hurt me, but he could break me. And that wouldn't be good.

Next to me, I saw Mookie open his mouth. That wouldn't be any good, either. Whatever he said would just get Ridley angry with both of us. I'd get broken and Mookie would get hurt.

The Lingering Stink

Mookie didn't say anything. Instead, he bent over and threw up—right between me and Ridley. It was an impressive spray. It hit the ground like it had been flung from a bucket. I jumped backwards, out of the splash zone. I looked away from the puke and looked back up at the other puke—namely, Ridley.

He was staring down, too. His face had gotten pale. He stepped back. Then he turned and walked off.

Wow—Ridley was grossed out by puke. Some people can't stand stuff like that. Some people faint if they see blood. I looked at the puddle. Ants were racing toward it. A swarm of flies landed and started chowing down.

Mookie might have lost his lunch, but the insect kingdom had found a feast.

"Who knew a big bully like Ridley would be such a wimp?" Abigail said.

"Yeah, especially about something that didn't bother me at all." I could take a bath in vomit and not care.

But even if I knew his weakness, that wouldn't help me the next time we met. I couldn't count on Mookie to throw up again. And I couldn't throw up at all. My body just didn't work that way anymore.

Before I could move, Rodney walked over. He got right in my face and poked my shoulder. "Stop trying to hang out with my brother. You're not his pal."

"Rodney, I think you should know—," I started to say.

"I mean it!" he yelled. "He's my brother. Mine. You can't be friends with him."

Man, he was too stupid. I tried again. "Look, Rodney—"

"Look, nothing." He poked me again. "I'm warning you."

"And I'm trying to tell you that you're standing in puke!" I shouted. I pointed down at his feet. "Look."

His eyes went wide and he backed up. I didn't know why Ridley was afraid of puke, but I guess Rodney was especially scared of it after what had happened in the high school gym when he'd tried to snap me in half. The memory of that moment still makes me smile.

He walked off almost as fast as Ridley, making gagging sounds.

"Ready for lunch?" Mookie asked.

"Lunch?" I stared at him. "You just puked."

"Yeah. So I've got lots of room. And it's taco day. Which means we can get all the salsa we want. How great is that? Come on. Let's go."

I followed Mookie to the cafeteria.

"I definitely feel better," he said as we got into the food line.

"I hope you aren't totally better," I said. "We might need you to puke again."

"I'll do my best. Hey, look, they have chicken fingers, too." He started to laugh as he loaded his tray.

"What's so funny?"

"I just realized something. If you put a finger down your throat, it makes you puke. But not a chicken finger. I wonder why."

"Maybe because you don't chew up your own fingers," I said.

"That's because I'm not a zombie." He held up his hands. "I chew my nails sometimes."

"Zombies don't chew their own fingers, either," I said.

"You're right. Wait—I think there's a joke in there somewhere," Mookie said. "You know, like the one about how you can pick your friends and pick your nose, but you can't pick your friend's nose. I got it! You can chew your nails and choose your friends, but you can't chew your friend's nails."

"Not bad." I had to admit, that was a pretty decent joke—especially compared with some of the ones he came up with.

When we got to our table, I noticed Adam had brought his lunch from home. I guess he didn't trust the cafeteria food after that stinky burger. I couldn't blame him. While I missed eating things like pizza and ice cream, I definitely didn't miss some of the stuff they cooked up in the cafeteria. From what I'd seen, the food at Borloff was pretty much the same as the food at Belgosi. They had smaller portions, but there was just as much slime, grease, gristle, and mystery.

After lunch, we headed back to class. I think everyone was tired of being crammed together. Even the teachers looked like they'd be happy when this was over.

Ridley gave me a mean look when he came in. But I managed to avoid him when we all headed out at the end of the day.

"Any appointments, shopping trips, or stuff like that?" I asked Mookie and Abigail when we got outside.

"Nope," they said.

"Great. I need somewhere to hang out," I said. "Bear Season is getting really unbearable."

"Let's go to my place," Abigail said. "I've got some new slides for my microscope."

"I thought you lost your microscope in the fire," I said. There'd been a fire at her house that destroyed all her stuff.

"Dr. Cushing sent me a new one. And a pair of binoculars."

"That's really nice of her." I'd introduced Dr. Cushing to Abigail, and they got along great. Dr. Cushing worked for BUM, but she wasn't a spy. She looked after the agents and did medical research.

"I've been bird-watching," Abigail said. "I saw three different types of hawks this week, and a pair of cardinals. Did you know there are flocks of land gulls near the mall parking lot?"

"Nope," I said. "I didn't even know there was any other kind of gull beside seagulls."

We headed over to Abigail's place. She told me a whole lot more about all kinds of birds. My favorite bird used to be turkey. With stuffing and gravy.

When Abigail paused to catch her breath, somewhere between finches and starlings, Mookie said, "How come Dr. Cushing never sends me anything?"

"What would you want her to send you?" Abigail asked.

"I don't know," Mookie said. "Maybe a laser or something cool. Yeah—a laser. That would be awesome." He swung his arms like he was using a light saber and made whooshing sounds.

"I don't think she has that kind of laser," Abigail said.

"Well, she should." Mookie kept swooshing. He didn't kill any space aliens, but he managed to knock over two garbage cans.

Then he started swooshing at me, yelling, "Zombie slicer! Off with his head!"

"Cut it out," I said.

That, of course, was the wrong thing to say.

"I can't cut it out," he said. "But I can cut it off."

For the rest of the walk, he kept slicing me with his imaginary laser, until I grabbed it from him and snapped it over my knee. "Enough!"

"Now you broke it," he said.

People might think you can't snap an imaginary object, but with Mookie's imagination, anything is possible.

Right after we got there, Abigail's mom brought glasses of lemonade up to her room. As she was handing out the drinks, she sniffed and said, "You might want to open a window. It's kind of stuffy in here."

She headed out. I sniffed. Something definitely smelled a bit ripe, like Adam's hamburger.

"Phew. Did one of your pet fish die?" Mookie asked.

"I don't have fish," Abigail said. "And I keep my room scrupulously clean."

"Something definitely smells rotten," Mookie said.

"It must be you guys," Abigail said. "Boys have been known to smell. Maybe you really do need to change your pants."

We both lifted our arms and smelled our pits. Mookie looked at Abigail. "It's not us," he said. "We didn't even have gym today. I'll bet it's you. Let's see." He walked toward her, sniffing like a rabbit.

"Keep your nose away from me," she said. "I don't smell. And there's no way I'm going to start sniffing myself."

"But something smells bad." I sniffed again. I'd found some bologna in the back of the fridge a year or two ago. It had fallen out of the deli drawer. I don't know how old it was, but it had smelled pretty much the same way as Abigail's room.

This didn't make sense. I looked at the perfectly level poster of Einstein on her wall, and the dust-free rows of books in her bookcase. Abigail was too neat to leave a sandwich lying under her bed or stick a hot dog in one of her desk drawers. Mookie had found a piece of hot dog under my bed once, but I'd never claimed to be all that neat and clean.

"Something in here has to be making that smell." I grabbed a stuffed animal from her bookcase. Her uncle had sent it to her from Bezimo Island. It was some kind of monkey creature with fangs and claws. It would probably give most kids nightmares, but I'd bet Abigail was fascinated by it.

I took a sniff. "Phew. Found it."

"No way," Abigail said. "Mr. Fangle doesn't smell." She snatched it from me and took a sniff, then wrinkled her nose. "Oh, ick." She tossed the stuffed animal out into the hall and closed the door.

Mookie sniffed. "I still smell it."

"How could you?" I asked.

Abigail sniffed the spot on the bookcase where the monkey had been. "It's fine. No smell." She stared at me. "Wait a minute. . . ."

"What?"

"You're not going to like this," she said.

I definitely didn't like the look in her eyes. It reminded me of the way parents' eyes get before they tell you bad news.

P (yo)U

"Hold out your hand," Abigail said.

I held out my hand. She sniffed it, then staggered back. "Ohmygosh! That's why my Mr. Fangle smelled." She snapped her fingers, then pointed at me. "And that's why Adam's burger smelled. Of course. This makes perfect sense. It's not either of those things. It's your hands."

"No way." I sniffed my fingers. Oh, no. She was right. My hands smelled like dead meat. I sniffed my arm. It was fine. "It's not all of me," I said. "I wonder if it's just my hands?" I looked at Mookie.

"Forget it!" he shouted. "I'm not sniffing your body."

"Check your feet," Abigail said.

I stared down at my feet. I guess I could try to get my foot close to my nose, but I didn't like the idea of bending my leg that much. I was afraid I'd snap it.

"Oh, just take off your shoe," Abigail said. "I'll do it."

I pulled off my shoe.

Abigail leaned over.

"That's disgusting," Mookie said.

"It's science," Abigail said. "We do what we have to in order to make discoveries. Madam Curie suffered a lot more than I ever will. But even she wouldn't eat a hamburger she sneezed on. So watch who you call disgusting." She sniffed my foot. Then she got up and sniffed my hand again. Finally, she sniffed the top of my head.

"Well?" I asked.

"Extremities," she said.

I waited.

"Hands and feet," she said. "Actually, probably just fingers and toes. The outer parts of your body are starting to rot."

"Rot!" I stared at my hands. I wanted to fling them off my arms. The bad thing was, I could probably do that with a hard-enough fling. "I'm rotting?"

"Well, you are a zombie," Mookie said. "So it's not like this is a gigantic surprise."

"But . . ." This was too big for my mind to swallow in one piece. I thought about the cover of Mookie's comic book, with all the badly rotted zombies. Bones broke through green flesh. Strips of skin hung from their faces, revealing cheeks and jaws. That couldn't be me. That would be terrible. I could hear the screams kids would make when they saw me. I'd be a real monster.

"Don't get upset," Abigail said. "It's obviously not happening quickly. And there's no visible sign of decomposition." She grabbed my left wrist and pushed my hand in front of my eyes. "See?"

I stared at my hand. It looked fine. A little pale, maybe, and a bit dry, but it wasn't green and drippy. There weren't any big hunks of flesh falling off.

"You aren't visibly rotting," she said.

"But my fingers smell," I said.

"It takes only a little bit of decay to create an odor," she said. "Just a handful of dead cells. That's one reason why clothing smells when it sits in a hamper for too long. It's not just from sweat. It's also got dead skin cells on it. Think about food wrappers in garbage cans."

"Mmmm," Mookie said. "Food wrappers. Yum. I love unwrapping food. Wrappers are fun to lick. Especially if there's melted cheese on them." He stuck out his tongue and licked the air. "Schnitzel Shack's Chili Cheese Dogs are great for that. So are Happy Cow's Triple Lard Bacon Burgers."

Mookie kept talking, listing his favorite wrappers. I

turned my attention back to Abigail. "I know what you mean. Sometimes when I take out the garbage, the stuff already out there gets pretty ripe. But even if it's just a little bit of rottenness right now, it's not going to get any better, right?"

She didn't answer me. I stared at her. She turned her head away. "Come on, Abigail. I need to know."

"You're right," Abigail said. "It won't get any better, unless we do something. But I can work on it. So can Dr. Cushing."

"Hey, so can I," Mookie said. "I'm still working on my research."

"I appreciate it," I said.

"And I'm working on other stuff, too," he said. "I'm always looking for things you can do with your zombie skills. You should be able to make tons of money."

Mookie's ideas always had problems. But I could tell he was trying to get my mind off my rotting body. "That's what makes you such an awesome friend," I said.

"I got another idea when we were walking here," Mookie said. "This is great."

"What?"

"Laser tag." He held up his hands like he was zapping someone. "You'd be awesome. Nobody could sneak up on you, and you could sneak up on everyone."

I guess he was right. I could look in two directions at

the same time. And people didn't sense me when I sneaked up on them, unless I made noise. "That could be pretty cool," I said.

Then I pictured myself in a dark room with a bunch of people running around and crashing into each other. Maybe laser tag wouldn't be such a good idea.

"Hey," Mookie said, "quarterbacks need to look all around, too." He threw an imaginary football. "And they make millions."

"That would give a whole new meaning to 'taking the snap,'" Abigail said. "One hard tackle, and you'd be flying in five different directions."

"Yeah. Facing a field of pro players would be ridiculous. I wouldn't even want to get on the field with an amateur like Ridley. You saw what he did with kids his own age."

Eventually, I knew I had to go home. As I was leaving, Abigail said, "Try not to worry, Nathan. People have dealt with much bigger problems than a little dead flesh."

"Thanks." I looked at my hands. They seemed fine. And the smell wasn't super noticeable yet. But if things got much worse, I wouldn't be able to go into a closed room without making everyone gasp and gag.

I guess Mookie knew what I was thinking. "Don't worry," he said. "I'll keep people from smelling you. Watch this." He scrunched up his face and hunched over.

"No!" Abigail and I both shouted.

"Save it for emergencies," I said.

With that, I headed home. When I got inside, I went right to the shower and scrubbed my hands and feet really well. I used lots of soap. After the shower, I smelled my fingers. They smelled like soap, along with the tiniest whiff of peaches, but I also caught a little bit of that dead-meat smell underneath all the other scents. It looked like I couldn't completely get rid of the smell. If it got much stronger, I'd be in real trouble. I dried myself off and went back downstairs.

Mom had gotten home. There was even more Bear Season stuff scattered around the house. Dad had stayed late at work, which meant I got to hear all the latest details from Mom.

Luckily, I managed to escape from her with the magic words, "I'd better do my homework."

That's about the only guaranteed way to escape a mom, except maybe for the ultimate sacrifice sentence: "I guess I'd better go clean my room."

I was actually so far ahead in my schoolwork that there wasn't much for me to do. Since I didn't sleep, I could read through my textbooks at night, and even do all the questions. I was building up so much extra credit, I'd probably still have some left when I got to high school.

I checked my e-mail that evening after Dad came

home. I figured, with him here for Mom to talk to, it was safe for me to go downstairs. I expected to find another message from BUM. But there wasn't anything. I hoped nothing had happened to Mr. Murphy. There were all sorts of groups of bad guys out there, and most of them would love to destroy BUM.

I checked my e-mail again right before I went to bed. Still nothing.

"Looking for a love letter?" Dad asked.

"No!"

He chuckled and walked away. Sometimes parents just didn't know when to stop joking.

I went up to my room and got ready for bed. Right after I turned off my lamp, I heard a loud pop. The plug flew out of the socket like the wall had spat it to the floor. Sparks shot from the outlet.

I'd survived one burning house. I didn't want to push my luck and go through that again. I rolled out of bed and tried to remember all the stuff my parents had drilled into me about fire safety. Go out the nearest window? Keep away from the window? Put out the fire. Don't put out the fire. It all jumbled up in my mind.

I had to do something. Fire and zombies are a bad combination.

10

Drop Everything

Before **I could** do anything about the fire, I realized the sparks weren't falling onto the carpet. They floated in the air, like baby fireflies. As more sparks shot out, they pulled together into letters and formed words. LOCAL PARK.

It was a message from Mr. Murphy. I knew that for sure, since several of the floating sparks exploded with small pops before their lights fizzled out. I watched the carpet to make sure it didn't burst into flame, then waited until my parents were in bed. I slipped out my window, climbed across the garage roof, and headed for the small park down the street from our house.

"What happened to e-mail?" I asked Mr. Murphy when I got there.

"Oh, Nathan, what fun is that? Really, you can't possibly pretend that you didn't enjoy our latest message. Hovering sparks. Brilliant, right?"

"Brilliant?" I couldn't believe he didn't see the danger. I gave it to him in simple words. "Sparks. Carpet. Wooden house. Boy who doesn't heal. Do you see a problem there?"

"There was absolutely no danger," he said. "That was a special low-temperature spark."

I joined him on the bench. I was still annoyed, but I could see that he'd never agree with me about the danger. "Maybe you can keep all the exploding stuff outside on the lawn."

"The sparks didn't really explode, did they?"

"Like popcorn," I said.

"All of them?"

"No. Just some."

"Well, the main thing is that you got the message. Let's get to work. This evening, I thought we'd . . ." He stopped and sniffed, glanced at the ground behind the bench, then got up and walked to the next bench. "People should be more careful where they discard the remains of their meals or walk their dogs."

I followed him and sat down. He sniffed again, then stared at me and raised one eyebrow.

"Yeah, it's me," I said.

"Have you abandoned bathing?" he asked.

"I'm rotting. But just a tiny bit. You can't even see anything." I thrust my hand toward his face.

He jerked away. Then he made a choking sound.

"Hey, it's not that bad."

He kept making the sound and shaking his head. Finally, I realized he was laughing. Mr. Murphy had sort of a sick sense of humor—especially when it came to stuff about me. He'd once told me that if my leg broke off, I shouldn't come running to him for help.

I figured the sooner we got it over with, the sooner we could get on with my lesson. "Whatever it is—just say it."

"That smell—you could call it a 'dead giveaway.'" He snorted for another minute. Then his face got serious. "I suppose we'll need to deal with this. We can't have you revealing your location to anyone with an unstuffed nose."

"I'm sure there's an answer," I said. I couldn't tell him Abigail was working on it. He had no idea my friends knew my secret, or knew I was working for BUM.

"I'll inform the lab," he said. "They'll get right on it. I'll tell Dr. Cushing, too. She's quite brilliant, in her own way. And I'll make sure we don't send you on any assignments where you could be sniffed out. Except by guard dogs, of course. They aren't interested in dead meat."

I thought about Spanky. "My neighbor's dog was all over me. He kept licking my hand."

"That's because he thought of you as food. Our pets would gleefully consume us if we let them. Guard dogs are trained not to eat anything that doesn't come from their handler. Otherwise, someone could slip them a sleeping pill."

That made sense. A guard dog couldn't guard anything if it was asleep. On the other hand, I didn't like the idea that everybody's pets would think of me as a snack.

"So, what am I learning tonight?" I asked.

He handed me a crumpled paper bag. "Throw this out, please."

"Sure." I walked over to the trash can near the road and tossed the bag. Then I went back to Mr. Murphy.

He took another paper bag out of his pocket. Then he reached into a different pocket and pulled out a stack of bills. I saw the one on top. Ben Franklin—it was a hundred.

"How much is that?" I asked.

"A lot." Mr. Murphy put the money in the bag, then handed it to me. "Place that in the trash can. Make sure nobody sees you."

"In the trash?"

He nodded. "A member of MI5, the British secret service, will be picking it up later."

"Really? Cool." I couldn't believe I was involved in an international plot. I went back to the trash can. I could feel the weight of the money in the bag. Man, I'd love to have just three or four of those bills. I could get an awesome game system with that. But I wasn't going to steal any money. And I wasn't going to let the wrong person get it. I checked all around before putting the bag in the trash. There was nobody in sight.

When I got back to Mr. Murphy, he said, "Go get both bags."

"What?"

"Get both bags."

I was starting to feel like a yo-yo. I got the bags and brought them back. Mr. Murphy patted the bench and said, "Have a seat."

Then he reached under the bench and pulled out a small camcorder. "Take a look. Here you are tossing some trash in the can."

I watched the video. It didn't show anything unusual. It was just a shot of me throwing out the first bag.

"Now, here you are, tossing a bag full of money."

I watched the second scene.

"See any difference?" Mr. Murphy asked.

"Maybe. I guess I looked sorta like I was kinda making sure nobody was around." Everything about me was weird in the second video. It was like I was doing something unnatural or illegal.

"Open the bags," Mr. Murphy said.

I did. They each had a wad of cash. He took the money and put it back in his pocket. "Nathan, when you thought you were tossing a bag of trash, you looked normal. When you knew you were tossing a bag of money, you didn't look natural. Spies are often called on to pick up or leave packages in places like trash cans. I think this is something you'll be good at, since you are capable of being dead calm." He chuckled after the last words, then added, "You just have to remember what you learned here."

"I will." I realized I had to pretend that whatever I was tossing was nothing but trash, even if I knew it was something valuable. I could do that.

He handed me a third bag. "Toss this one."

"Is it money or trash?" I asked.

"It doesn't matter. You often won't know what you're dropping. Or why."

I took the bag and tossed it into the can. I tried my best to act like it was just trash.

When I got back, Mr. Murphy said, "Well done. That was an easier lesson than some of them."

"At least I wasn't in danger of being ripped apart by guard dogs."

He smiled. "Who knows? The night is far from over."

But there weren't any dogs to worry about. We actually spent another hour talking about spycraft, and about some of the things I read in the book he'd given me. He might have been weird in a lot of ways, but he was actually a pretty good teacher.

I was all alone for breakfast again the next morning. It was Wednesday, so I guess Mom was excited about all the Bear Season stuff that was supposed to arrive. That was fine. I was old enough to take care of myself— especially since I didn't actually need to eat. And it made me feel grown up knowing my parents trusted me.

I crossed the street as soon as I left my house, so Spanky wouldn't be tempted to munch on my fingers or toes. He looked at me from the edge of his lawn. I'd have to remember to pick up a dog treat for him. I had a feeling he wouldn't care if it smelled like my hands.

"I talked to Uncle Zardo last night," Abigail said when I got to school.

"How's he doing?"

"Good. He's still on Bezimo Island. Anyhow, I told him about your problem, and he's sure he can help."

"Really?"

"Yup. He's getting right to work on Stink-Be-Gone."

"No!" I got in Abigail's face. "No more formulas. Especially not from your uncle. The last one killed me. This one would probably make my nose fall off."

"Maybe you're right," Abigail said. "He does tend to get unexpected results whenever he goes into a lab. But I think it was sweet that he wanted to help."

The bell rang before I could tell her that *sweet* was the last word I'd use to describe her uncle. We headed inside.

On the way to class, Mookie said, "I think I found another cure last night. I was reading *Zombie Surfer*. It's an awesome comic. Anyhow, in issue thirty-seven, they cure this zombie with a brain transplant."

"No! Forget it."

"But it makes sense. We can put your brain in another body. Wait—maybe we need to put another brain in your body. I can't remember which way it was." He turned to Abigail. "Does Nathan need a new brain or a new body?"

"Both," she said. "Or neither. You, on the other hand, need a new brain and new intestines."

"And you need to keep looking," I told Mookie. "I'm planning to keep my body and my brain."

By then, we'd reached our classroom. If I thought

Bear Season was bad, I was about to get hit by a second wave of unbearable cuteness. Right after we took our seats, there was an announcement calling us down the hall for an assembly.

"I hope it's a magic show," Mookie said. "I love magic shows."

"Why would it be a magic show?" I asked. I figured it was probably something about being careful crossing the street. Or maybe there'd be some guys dressed up as presidents, reading speeches and telling us to follow our dreams.

We moved through the mobbed hallways to the cafetorium. Belgosi had a real auditorium, but Borloff just had a stage at the end of the cafeteria. No chairs, either. They'd been stacked, and the tables had all been folded up. We had to sit on the floor.

"This is going to be tight," Mookie said.

He wasn't kidding. By the time we'd all been wedged together on the floor, I wasn't sure where I ended and he began. I was afraid if he farted, I'd be forced to burp.

Right after we all got seated, a woman who had way too big a smile got on the stage and leaned toward the microphone.

"Well, isn't it a pleasure to see so many lovely faces," she said.

"That's Mrs. Matheson," Abigail whispered. "I had her for kindergarten. She's pretty nice."

"Yeah, I remember her now." I'd had Mrs. Morlock, but I remembered how Mrs. Matheson was always singing to her class and playing a zither.

"We brought you here to tell you something very exciting." Her smile grew even wider. "As you know, each year my kindergarten class puts together a parade. This year, we have a special theme—our forest friends. The parents have worked very hard to make the costumes."

She turned toward the side of the stage and clapped her hands. Little forest creatures—okay, actually little kids dressed like forest creatures—wobbled out from the side and formed a crooked line across the stage. It was obvious that some parents were a lot better at costumes than others. There were all kinds of critters. Squirrels, rabbits, deer, and, of course, bears. I could just hear how Mom would squeal if she saw this.

"Because we have so many special guests in our school, we've decided to let another grade take part in the parade," she said. The smile reached what I felt was an impossible width.

"Not us," Mookie said. "Please, not us."

"There are eight grades in the building to choose from," Abigail said. "So the chance of it being us is only twelve and a half percent. I think it would be fun. Look how cute they are."

Mrs. Matheson waited until the talking stopped, then said, "Our special friends for our forest animals will be the eighth grade."

A groan rose up from behind us. I looked back. You would have thought all the kids had suddenly been forced to bite into a lemon. Or a tiny forest creature. Ridley was actually snarling. I hoped the animal parade didn't turn into a hunting trip.

"This is going to end badly," Abigail said.

"At least we aren't involved," I said.

But I got involved in something else during recess.

11

Unwanted Attention

Recess started out fine. We'd gotten used to hanging out by the back of the school, watching the other kids. But about ten minutes after Abigail, Mookie, and I sat down, Ferdinand got whacked in the head with a kickball while he was walking near the field. The *bwoink!* sound of an overinflated red rubber ball smacking against a skull echoed across the playground.

Ferdinand staggered a couple steps. Kids all over the field watched him. Including Ridley.

"Oh, no," Abigail said. "He's like a shark that smells blood in the water."

I watched Ferdinand wander too close to Ridley.

Before we could yell a warning, Ridley grabbed Ferdinand's foot, lifted him up in the air, and started shaking him.

"I have to stop this," I said. "The bell isn't going to save him this time."

Abigail grabbed my arm. "Wait. Let the other eighth-graders handle it."

I scanned the playground. Kids were watching. But just like last time, nobody moved toward Ridley. Not even the kids who'd stopped the game of catch-the-fourth-grader the other day. "They're afraid of him. It's up to me."

I trotted across the playground. I heard Mookie and Abigail hurrying to catch up with me.

Am I crazy?

Maybe I was. But somebody had to do something. And Abigail was right—I'd faced deadly enemy spies and monsters. I should be able to handle Ridley. When I got close—but not so close that he could reach me—I shouted. "Hey! Put him down!"

Ridley, who looked as happy as a baby with a rattle, turned toward me. His smile grew dangerous. "Sure, Peach Boy."

He lifted his arm higher. Ferdinand, who was letting out squeals the human ear could barely hear, rose so high, his head was even with mine. "Down you go." Ridley opened his fingers one at a time until Ferdinand dropped from his grip.

He hit the ground with a thud and lay there like he'd just been rammed by a car. But he was breathing, so I figured he might be okay.

"You're dead," Ridley said.

I'd heard the same words from his brother more than once. Neither of them had a clue how true that was.

Ridley took a step toward me.

Next to me, Mookie jammed two fingers down his throat. I waited. Nothing happened.

He shoved fingers from both hands down his throat. He looked like a magician struggling to pull a rabbit from an unlikely place.

Still nothing.

Ridley glanced toward Mookie for a moment, then looked back at me.

Mookie pulled his hands from his mouth. "Guess I should've had more breakfast."

"Violence never solved anything," Abigail said.

Ridley lunged for me.

"Get help," I whispered to Abigail. I turned and ran. I'm not superfast. But I was pretty sure I could outrun a guy Ridley's size. All I had to do was keep out of his reach until he got tired. Of course, if he caught me, he'd tire himself out throwing punches.

So I needed to make absolutely sure he wouldn't catch me. I ran straight for the monkey bars. When I reached them, I grabbed a bar and used it to swing left in a sharp turn. I heard Ridley skitter and slide as he tried to keep up.

Good. He wasn't able to change direction quickly. I figured a guy that size would move like a supertanker.

I shot toward the swings and used one of the legs to make another turn, to the right this time. I didn't risk looking over my shoulder. I could tell from the sound of his feet slapping on the ground that he hadn't gotten any closer. He wouldn't be able to catch me, as long as I didn't stop. Now all I needed to do was keep running until help came. I decided not to use any more of the playground equipment.

I headed around the side of the school. Ridley was still behind me. I ran a loop all the way around the building. Kids were watching us. It reminded me of one night when Dad and I saw a TV show where a crocodile was hunting a zebra. You just knew it was going to end badly for the zebra. That's what all the kids expected. They figured Ridley would catch me and tear me to pieces. As far as they were concerned, he was an eighth-grader and I was just a little kid.

I didn't see Abigail. That was good. She'd gone to get a teacher. I couldn't send Mookie. Guys can't snitch. You do it once, you get a reputation. But it was fine for Abigail to go get help.

On my second lap, I could tell that Ridley was losing his breath. He was huffing like someone trying to get a campfire started from a glowing stick. When we got back to the playground, I was happy to see Principal Ambrose standing by the back door.

"Hold it, you two! What's going on?"

I skidded to a halt in front of him and put my hands behind my back.

"We were playing tag," Ridley said between gasps as he caught his breath. He glared at me, daring me to call him a liar. "Our teachers told us to play games with the younger students."

I was going to explain that it wasn't a game, but the principal was way ahead of me. "I remember you," he said to Ridley. "You spent a lot of time in my office. You keep your hands off these students. If you so much as touch one of them, you'll face criminal charges."

Wow. I never thought Principal Ambrose would come down so hard on Ridley. But that was great. Ridley wouldn't dare touch me—or anyone else—after that warning.

"Go back inside," Principal Ambrose said.

Ridley slunk off. I was about to thank the principal when he spun toward me and said, "As for you, I don't know what you did to instigate this, but I'll be keeping my eye on you." He looked from me to Mookie and then back. I saw a glimmer in his eyes. He had to have remembered the last time he'd seen us, back in the Belgosi boys' room, the day I realized something was really wrong with me. "I mean it," he said. Then he walked off.

"Thanks," I said to Abigail.

"It was nothing. Just try to stay away from him."

"That's my plan." I looked around for Ferdinand. He was back on his feet. He was a bit wobbly, but didn't seem to be in pain. "Come on," I said to Mookie and Abigail. I headed back toward the swings.

"Why are we going there?" Mookie asked.

"So you can help me find my fingers." I held up my right hand. My index and middle finger had snapped off when I'd swung around the leg. I hadn't even felt it, but I'd seen them go flying.

After we found the fingers, we took them over to the side of the school so nobody would hear my screams. The only time I feel pain is when I glue pieces back on. It doesn't hurt for long, but it hurts a lot.

"Sorry I couldn't puke when you needed me to," Mookie said when we got back to the playground. I don't know why it didn't work." He jammed a finger back down his throat.

Someone smacked my shoulder. "Hey! I warned you not to play with my brother."

I turned and found myself facing Rodney.

Before I could say anything, Mookie, who still had his fingers down his throat, made a gagging sound, bent halfway over, and hurled right in my direction. I managed to leap out of the way.

Rodney wasn't so lucky. He got nailed right across his shirt. He looked down, screamed, and ran off.

"Hmmm," Mookie said after he wiped his mouth with his sleeve. "It's working now."

The lunch bell rang.

"The bugs are getting another feast." Abigail pointed to the part of Mookie's latest deposit that had managed to reach the ground. "I, on the other hand, seem to have lost my appetite."

"I'll eat your lunch if you don't want it," Mookie said. "I'm really starving now."

"Hey, I'm just glad there's no way Ridley can hurt me," I said. I figured I was safe from Rodney for a while, too. The last time he'd been nailed this way, he'd stayed out of school for a week.

"Don't be so sure you're safe from Ridley," Mookie said. "A guy like him, he'll try to find a way to get even."

"I'm not worried. At least he won't be there at lunch." That was true. But after lunch, we had gym. Ridley wasn't just there—he was there with a plan.

When we got out to the field, Ridley glared at me. Then his jaw started moving up and down, like he was chewing a really tough piece of beef jerky.

"He looks like a cow," Mookie said.

"Except bigger." Then I saw something that worried me. There was a flicker of light in his eyes—the sort of spark you see when someone gets an idea. One side of his mouth curled up into a sneer.

"Hey, Coach," Ridley said.

"What do you want, Mule?"

I guess that was Mr. Scotus's nickname for Ridley.

Ridley pointed right at our cluster of fifth-graders. "How about we play against them. That would toughen them up. Make real men out of them."

"Yeah," the kid next to him said.

"Let's do it!" another larger creature shouted.

All of them joined in.

"We are so dead," Mookie said. "Especially you. I know you're already dead, but after this, you'll be like double dead."

Nearby, I heard a sound like crickets. I looked over at Ferdinand. He was trembling so hard, he was sending out sound waves.

I pointed toward Mr. Scotus. "He won't let it happen. We'll be okay."

We all watched Mr. Scotus. He also did the chewing thing for a moment. Then he got the same evil smile as Ridley. I realized that Mr. Scotus was the sort of person kids like Ridley turned into when they grew up.

I was wrong. We were definitely doomed.

12

Horsing Around

Just when **I** figured my body was about to be crushed like walnut shells on the football field, Mr. Lomux, of all people, said, "No way."

Every head in the class turned toward him. "He's my hero," Mookie whispered. "I'll never try to make his veins pop again."

But our rescue didn't last very long. "My kids need to earn the right to play yours," Mr. Lomux said. "We'll play fifth against fifth, and eight against eighth. The winners will play on Friday. Okay—choose up sides. Mort, Steven, you're captains."

As we waited to get picked, I knew two things:

Whichever eighth-grade team had Ridley would win, and whichever fifth-grade team had to play against him on Friday would do more than just lose—they'd get broken into pieces. Especially me.

"I'll take Ferdinand," Mort said.

"I've got Dilby," Steven said.

Everyone, including Ferdinand and Dilby, froze for a moment. Then I realized what was happening. Mort and Steven both wanted to lose.

"This is amazing," Mookie said as the picking continued.

"It's like Opposite Day," I said. The kids who always got picked last—and I knew all about how that felt—were getting picked first. I'd lost my spot as last-pick right after I became half-dead, so I got scooped up in the middle.

I ended up on Mort's team. "Nobody score," he said as we huddled.

"We have to do more than that," I said. "We have to make sure they score."

"I've got that covered," Mort said.

He took the hike and threw a hard pass right at Adam, who was on the other team. As the ball hit Adam in the chest, he clutched at it. Then he stared in horror. But Mort rushed over and touched him before he could drop the ball. We'd managed to turn it over on the first play.

Steven took the snap, then dropped the ball. Everyone stood there.

"Play!" Mr. Lomux screamed. "Start playing or you'll do five thousand push-ups every class for the rest of the year."

Seven veins bulged on his shiny bald head.

Both sides tried to make it look like we were playing for real, but we were all trying to lose. Finally, around the middle of the period, Mort got a great idea. He stood way back, took the hike, then dashed the wrong way and fell down in our end zone.

He didn't need to be touched. In our gym-class rules, a play ended if the ball carrier hit the ground. The other team scored a safety. We were down two to nothing.

Of course, on the next play, the other team did the same thing, tying the score at 2–2. With a long shotgun hike, there was no way anyone could catch the quarterback before he reached the wrong end zone.

It was our turn again. That was good. I realized, since our side had thought of it first, we'd either win or tie, depending on when the period ended. Things were looking up.

"Time out!" Mr. Lomux screamed. He stormed over to Mr. Scotus and started talking.

The girls, who were resting after running laps, were

watching us. Abigail wandered over to me and Mookie. "What's happening?"

I explained how we were each trying to lose.

"Interesting," she said. "It's like the puzzle of the slower horse."

I waited for her to explain what she meant. "It's a classic problem. A man has two sons. Each son owns one horse. In his will, the man leaves all his money to whichever son has the slower horse. So they have a race, but both sons just sit there on the horses." She pointed at our two teams. "Same thing."

"So what did they do?" I asked.

Abigail shook her head. "Nope. I'm not telling you. You can figure this one out. It's not that hard. If I always give you the answers, your brain will get lazy."

I thought for a moment. Then I saw it. "They switch horses!"

"Right," Abigail said. "Now, each one wants to race fast on his brother's horse so his own horse is slower."

"Huh?" Mookie said. "I don't see what that has to do with us."

"I'll tell you later." I pointed at the gym teachers. "The important thing is that *they* don't figure it out." And that looked like a safe bet. Mr. Lomux and Mr. Scotus were both scratching their heads and talking.

"It's sort of like watching two mules trying to solve an algebra problem," Abigail said.

"It is kind of sad," I said.

A second later, Mookie shouted, "I get it! I get it!"

Everyone looked at him. Then, before I could clamp a hand on his mouth, he yelled, "It's a good thing they're not making our losing team play their winner."

Oh, no . . . I watched the teachers. Maybe they still wouldn't catch on. My hopes vanished when they stopped scratching their heads. They talked. They nodded. Mr. Lomux came over and pointed at us. "Fifth-grade losers play the eighth-grade winners."

We fought hard. But we lost. Across the field, I kept watching Ridley hammering the kids on the opposite team. One kid got knocked right out of his sneakers.

"We have two days to live," I said as we walked off the field.

"Maybe I'll be sick that day," Mookie said.

"I wish I could do that." My mom totally overreacted any time I got sick: I couldn't risk another trip to the doctor. I'd been lucky enough to get through the last one.

13

Costume foolery

Mom was in the living room when I came home from school, sitting on the couch. That was weird. She should have been at work. When I got closer, I saw she'd been crying.

"What's wrong?" I asked. I wasn't too worried. Mom cries pretty easily. Dad and I won't even stay in the living room when there's a sad movie on. If something really bad had happened—like when my hamster died—she would have been waiting by the door for me.

"Nothing," she said. She sniffed, then wiped her nose with a tissue.

"Is everyone okay?"

She nodded. "Everything's fine. I just made a mistake at work."

"Hey, everyone makes mistakes," I said.

"Not like this." She reached over and picked up something from the couch. She held it up. It was big, floppy, and sort of shapeless.

"What's that?" It was Wednesday, which meant the bear outfits had arrived at the store. But the thing in her hand couldn't possibly be one of those.

"It's supposed to be a Stuffy Wuffy Jammy Bear outfit. I ordered the wrong size." She held up a bear. Then she draped the pajamas over it. The bear looked like it was inside a tent. The hood, all by itself, was bigger than the bear. "It's the first time they ever let me order the outfits, and I made a huge mistake on the computer. I hate those little drop-down windows where you have to click on a choice. They always seem to change when I'm not looking."

I tried to think what Abigail would do. "Can't you get larger bears?" I asked.

"Nobody wants bears that big," she said. "They'd be huge.

I noticed there was other stuff piled on the couch. "What's with the wings?" The instant I said that, and heard Mom's gasp, I felt bad.

"I messed up that, too," she said. "I'm so bad with computers."

I couldn't argue with that. The one time Mom had tried to order a pair of shoes online, she'd ended up getting fifteen pounds of potato salad delivered to the house. Dad and I were never able to figure out exactly how she had managed to do that. Actually, even though he works with numbers, Dad isn't all that much better than Mom when it comes to going online. That sort of stuff is best left for kids, since we understand the Internet.

"Are those the angel wings?" I asked.

Mom nodded. "Wrong size. Wrong shape."

I could see that. They looked more like they belonged to wasps than to angels. Giant wasps. Stingy Bear? No—that wouldn't be a big seller. Most people didn't like insects. There was something else on the couch. It was about the size of a silver dollar, but shaped like a flat gem. I guess Mom had messed up a bit with the decorations for Diamond Jewel Bear, too. I didn't ask.

This was bad. I really wanted to help. "Maybe you can shrink the pajamas."

Mom shook her head. "It's not cotton or wool. It won't shrink."

Man, solving problems was hard. I made a few more suggestions, but none of them were any good either. In the end, all I could do was say the sort of thing Mom would say to me if I messed up. "It will work out okay. You'll see."

She nodded, but I could tell she didn't feel that way.

I was still thinking about Mom's problem after bedtime, when two chipmunks ran up the phone pole outside my window, holding a flashing sign that read GO TO BUM.

One of them slipped off the pole and plunged to the ground. It hit the curb and exploded. The other one managed to climb down.

As usual, I slipped out after my parents had gone to bed, and headed to the museum.

When I got off the elevator on the other side, Mr. Murphy said, "Good news, Nathan. You don't have to be a little stinker."

"Very funny. What did you come up with?"

"I'll let Professor Quirlian tell you himself," Mr. Murphy said. "I don't want to spoil his surprise."

"Professor Quirlian?" I asked.

"The greatest scientist on our staff," Mr. Murphy said. "Perhaps the greatest espionage engineer ever. Come on, it's time you met him."

I followed Mr. Murphy down the hall. We went into an elevator, but not the kind that took us to other towns and cities. This was a normal one that went down. There weren't any numbers on it for the floors. We seemed to move for a long while. "How deep is this place?" I asked.

"Nobody knows," Mr. Murphy said.

The door opened and I followed him out. We went down a short hall that ended by a double door. I read the writing on the small sign next to the door: R&D

"R and D?" I asked.

"Research and Development," Mr. Murphy said. "This is where the magic happens."

"And the explosions?" I asked.

"Knock it off. We don't have that many explosions."

"Yeah, right," I said. "Nothing blows up more than once."

Mr. Murphy ignored that. As he reached for the door, he said, "Nathan, this is our most top secret area. Very few people have been allowed in here. You must swear to me that you will never mention what you see to anyone."

"Sure. I can keep a secret. I've been keeping a huge one for a while now."

"Good point." He opened the door, let me go first, and followed me in. I froze for a moment when I saw it was a lab. I still remembered every detail of the lab where I'd been splashed with Hurt-Be-Gone and turned into a zombie. That was at Romero Community College. This lab was a lot bigger. It was actually larger than my school's gym.

A guy scurried up to us. He was really old, and sort of bent over, like the lady down the street from me who owns all the cats. Except he wasn't covered with cat hair. He flashed me a huge smile.

"Professor Quirlian," Mr. Murphy said, "this is our newest agent—Nathan Abercrombie. He's starting to smell."

"Wait! Solution!" Professor Quirlian skittered across the lab and grabbed something, then hurried back to me. "Brilliant! Totally brilliant." He handed me a cotton ball. "Here. Sniff."

I took a sniff. That was a mistake. I felt like I'd been drop-kicked in the gut by a moose. The cotton ball smelled like someone had taken a dead woodchuck, stuffed it with pus and tuna salad, and left it in a warm place for a month. "That's awful!"

"Certainly. Stunningly awful. But now—observe."

He dashed across the lab to a workbench and picked up a beaker. That was another thing I didn't like seeing. It was a large glass jar of Hurt-Be-Gone that turned me into a half-dead zombie. I decided to stay where I was, safely across the room.

Professor Quirlian grabbed some tongs and plunged the cotton ball in the liquid, then pulled it out, puffed on it a couple times, and raced back to me.

"Again," he said, thrusting the cotton ball in my face.

"No thanks."

He waggled the tongs and gave me a goofy smile. "Trust me."

I sniffed. Nothing. "It doesn't stink. Cool—you've got something that kills odors?" I wouldn't mind dipping my hands in that stuff if it kept me from stinking.

"No. Better. Look closely." He raised the ball to my eye. "Encased. Brilliant? Yes?"

I squinted at the cotton ball. Tiny rainbows shimmered across the surface. I touched it. Weird. It was covered in a superthin film of some kind. "Plastic?" I asked.

"Yes, polymer," he said. He pointed at my head and then lowered his hand toward my feet. "Covered. Head to toe. No more stink."

"Uh, yeah." I thought about getting my body coated in plastic. It didn't seem like a great idea. Rotting didn't seem like a great idea either, but I had no idea what the plastic would do to me. What if it started to shrink? Or what if I could never get it off? "I'll think about it."

I left the lab. Mr. Murphy met me outside and took me back up to his level. Before I returned to the museum, I dropped in on Dr. Cushing.

"Any luck with the bone machine?" I asked her. She'd been working on a machine that would make my bones absorb calcium so they wouldn't break so easily.

"I'm making progress," she said.

"So the test pig isn't exploding anymore?" The bone machine had a bit of a bad—and messy—side effect.

"No. Not the whole thing. Just the head."

"Well, I guess that's progress," I said. "What about this?" I held up my hand and wrinkled my nose.

"I have some ideas," she said.

"But no solution yet?"

"No. I'm sorry. I know this is hard on you. I wish I could just flip a switch and fix everything. Science doesn't work that way."

"I know that for sure," I said. "I have Abigail around to remind me. But I guess I'm pretty lucky to have both of you working on my problems."

"And we're pretty lucky to have such a brave subject," she said.

"I'm not that brave," I said. "I really don't have much choice."

"Nathan, I've seen what you can do. You're the bravest young man I've ever met. Even most adults would give up if they were in your situation. Don't ever think you lack courage."

"Thanks." It's a good thing zombies can't blush.

We chatted for several more minutes. Then I left. On the way home, I kept staring at my hands. And I kept sniffing them. *Rotting.*

I remember hearing kids shout, "You stink!" at other kids. That was something lots of kids said. I'm sure I'd yelled it often enough. But in my case, it was going to take on a whole new meaning.

I went back home and sat in bed, staring at the wall. Then I got up and wandered around my room. There was something behind my bookcase. Right. I'd forgotten all about it.

I pulled the notebook out and flipped through my drawings. Back when I first became a zombie, I'd wanted to use my powers to become a superhero. I'd even come up with a costume. But real life, and my role as a spy, had taken over. Still, it was fun to look at the sketches and imagine saving people from burning buildings or floods. It took my mind off my rotting flesh for a while.

14

Let's Not Be Shellfish

Mom **didn't leave** for work early the next morning. When I came down, she was just sitting at the breakfast table, sipping tea and looking sad.

"Don't you need to get ready for the big day?" I asked.

She shook her head. "It's not going to be that big, thanks to me."

"Come on, you've got all sorts of cool bears. I really like the baseball one. Philly Bearster—that's an awesome name."

"You think so?"

I nodded. "Totally." That was one of the costumes

she'd gotten right. "There are tons of Phillies fans around here."

She took a sip of tea. "It is kind of nice. I think we'll sell a lot of them. I just wish we weren't stuck with all those mistakes of mine."

"It will work out," I said. It felt so strange saying parent-type stuff to my mom. But she and Dad had done that for me all my life, even when I'd messed up really badly, so I guess it was nice I had a chance to return the favor. Not that anything I did could make a difference.

"Thanks, Nathan," she said when I headed out.

"Sure."

Mookie acted weird from the moment I saw him outside of school. He kept looking at me and grinning.

"What?" I finally asked him when we were heading to the cafeteria.

"I've got a big surprise for you after school," he said. "It's huge. Gigantic. Enormous. The best thing ever."

"Tell me about it."

"We're going to— Hey, wait. You can't trick me that easily. If I tell you now, it won't be a surprise."

I looked over at Abigail. She shrugged. I guess she didn't have any idea what it was either.

I tried to get it out of him a couple more times, but he just kept saying, "Sorry. I'm going to clam up." Then he'd laugh, like that was some sort of joke.

Finally, after school, he said, "Come on. It's not far."

He jogged off down the sidewalk toward town. Abigail and I followed him.

"Any ideas?" I asked her.

"Not when Mookie is involved," she said. "It could be anything from a birthday party to a giant hole in the ground."

"It's not my birthday," I said.

"I don't think that matters when Mookie is involved," she said. "Maybe his mom won more cupcakes."

"I hope not. They'd probably be made with lettuce or something like that."

Mookie was half a block away. He looked back and waved us forward. "Come on. We're almost there." He went around the corner.

He was waiting for us by a parking lot near the next corner.

"No way," I said when I saw the sign.

"Come on," Mookie said. "You can win. And the prize is five hundred dollars."

I looked at the sign in front of the seafood store. OYSTER-EATING CONTEST! BIG CASH PRIZES!

"Mookie, do you remember what happened when you talked me into the chicken-wing-eating contest?"

He nodded. "Yeah. That was awesome."

"Awesome? Are you kidding? I went around for a

week with sixty-three wings rotting in my stomach. And then I nearly killed a whole gym full of parents. I wouldn't call that awesome."

"I would." He pointed at the sign. "It's oysters. There's no way they'd get stuck inside of you." He turned toward Abigail. "Right?"

"They are sort of slimy," she said. "I guess they'd slip out as easily as they went in. Especially if you didn't chew them."

"No! Not you, too. You can't think this is a good thing." I figured she'd help me convince Mookie this was a terrible idea.

"It's easy money," she said. "You can buy an awesome video game system with it, and some cool games, and a second controller so you can play games with your best friend in the universe. And you'll even have some money left over for chocolate."

"And licorice," Mookie said. "Pretzels, too."

I opened my mouth to protest, but Abigail held up her hand. "Think about it logically for a second. The oysters slide right in. Later, they slide right out. What could go wrong?"

"Yeah," Mookie said. "It's perfect. I even checked the rules. There's no junior division. So when you win, you get the big prize."

I guess Abigail had a point. The only reason I had trouble with the wings was that the meat got jammed inside me and I couldn't get it out. But oysters wouldn't be a problem. Back when I was alive, I never would have eaten one. Not even for five hundred dollars. But now, I barely tasted stuff. And nothing made me feel sick. Mookie was right—that money would be enough to get an awesome gaming system and a bunch of games. "Sure. Let's do it."

I went into the store and signed up for the contest. The guy stared at me, but didn't stop me. I saw some of the same people who'd been at the chicken-wing contest. I guess that shouldn't be a surprise. It took a special kind of person to stuff his gut over and over. Speaking of which, down at the competition table, I spotted the biggest guy I'd ever met.

"Hey, kid," Bubba Chompsketski said. He waved and pointed to the seat next to him. "Good to see you."

I went over. "Hi, Bubba. Been doing a lot of this?"

He nodded. "Every contest around. Not only do I make good money, but I also get lots of free food. Do you like oysters?"

"Not really," I said.

He shook his head. "Me neither. But every athlete has to make sacrifices for his sport."

The judges put a plate of oysters in front of me. I still couldn't believe people thought of them as food. They reminded me of something you'd find splattered across your hand after a really hard sneeze. When the contest started, I began slurping oysters as fast as I could. Abigail was right—they slid right down without any trouble. The pile of empty shells in front of me grew into a mountain. Next to me, Bubba was keeping up the pace. It was close. But when they blew the whistle and counted the shells, I'd won by seven and a half oysters. I'm happy to say, I wasn't the one who ate a half.

"Nicely done," Bubba said, holding out a hand dripping with oyster juice.

"Thanks." We shook. My hand vanished inside his hand, but he didn't squeeze hard.

As soon as I got my prize money, in the form of five hundred-dollar bills, I turned to Mookie and Abigail. "Okay—let's get this stuff out of me." My stomach bulged against my pants, but the button didn't break.

"See, it was a great idea," Mookie said when we left the store. "You can tell me I'm brilliant. I won't let it go to my head."

I had to admit he was right. For once, his idea had been perfect. "You're brilliant, Mookie."

"I know," he said. "It's a gift. But one I plan to use to help others."

"The sun was shining brightly," Abigail said as we headed for the playground behind Borloff Lower Elementary. "Shining with all its might."

I gave her a puzzled look, because it was actually sort of cloudy, but she kept on talking. I realized she was telling us a poem about oysters. It was actually pretty cool.

When we reached the playground, we went to the monkey bars. As I climbed up, I could feel gravity trying to pull me to the ground, along with all the oysters. That was good. In a moment, once I'd flipped over, gravity would drain the oysters from me.

I hooked my legs over one of the bars and hung down. Then I opened my mouth and nodded. Mookie and Abigail put their hands on my stomach and started pushing.

Please work, I thought. There was nothing more awful than the idea of having tons of oysters stuck in my stomach. I had a feeling they'd smell way worse than chicken if they started to rot.

Plop!

Something hit the ground beneath me with the sound of a wet washcloth smacking a shower floor. Good. It was working.

Plop-a-plop-a-ploppity-plop.

More stuff hit. Mookie and Abigail pushed harder. Oysters poured out of my mouth. I felt like a fountain.

"See? It's working just fine," Mookie said.

"No trouble at all," Abigail said.

"I think that's the last one," Mookie said. "I should have brought a video camera. I'd bet we could have sold a video of that. It was almost like a magic trick. Hey— imagine how awesome it would look if we played it backwards."

"Squawk," Abigail said.

Squawk? No, it wasn't Abigail. I saw motion out of the corner of my eye.

"Seagulls!" Mookie screamed.

"Land gulls," Abigail said. "Not that it matters." She ducked and covered her head as the birds swooped down. In seconds, the gulls dived at us from all over the sky, tearing into the pile of oysters. I wrapped my arms around my head to protect my eyes.

It was like being inside a giant feather pillow in the middle of a pillow fight.

I was surrounded by flaps and squawks. But above all that, I could hear Mookie's and Abigail's shrieks.

Finally, the birds fluttered off. I looked at the ground beneath me. All the oysters were gone. But the birds had left something else behind. I stared at Mookie and Abigail for a moment. Then I checked my own clothes. All three of us were splattered from head to toe. We had a lot of feathers stuck to us, too.

I got off the monkey bars.

What could go wrong? That's what Mookie had asked. I glared at him.

He shrugged. "I never thought—"

"Shut up," I told him.

"Maybe we could go to a car wash," he said.

I looked over at Abigail. I expected her to turn this into some sort of science lesson. But she just shuddered and said, "I need to go home."

"We all do," I said.

I figured I could get home before my parents, but Dad was already there. He stared at me for a moment. "What happened to you?"

"I tried bird-watching," I said. "It seemed like it would be interesting."

"Oh. Was it?"

"Nah. It was sort of messy. I think I got too close."

"I can see that. You'd better wash up before your mom gets home."

"Good idea."

He sniffed. "I didn't think bird droppings smelled that bad. Make sure you scrub."

"I will." I sniffed. I could smell it, too. My own rotting stink was outsmelling whatever the land gulls had produced. And they ate garbage and fish guts. So, basically, my hands smelled worse than digested garbage. It didn't get much lower than that.

I headed for the stairs. But then I turned back. "Mom's really upset about this costume stuff."

Dad nodded. "She loves her job. This is pretty hard on her. But she'll get over it. We just have to be supportive."

"Do you think they'll fire her?"

"I hope not."

"Yeah. Me, too." As much as the whole bear thing was way too cute for me, I knew it was important to my mom. "Did you see the big pair of pajamas?"

"It was definitely large," Dad said.

"I didn't laugh. Not even once, the whole time she was showing stuff to me."

"Good boy."

I went upstairs and took a long shower. I also spent a long time thinking. I realized I had to decide whether to take Professor Quirlian up on his offer to coat me in his plastic formula, at least until Abigail and Dr. Cushing figured out a better solution. I didn't want to do it. But if I hoped to keep people from figuring out I was dead, it might be my best choice.

When I came back downstairs, Mom was home. I thought she'd be moping around. But Sad Mom had been replaced by Annoyed Mom. This was not a good trade. She gave me that stare. I'd done something wrong. I thought back through the day. As far as I could remember, I hadn't done anything bad. I'd folded my clean clothes and put them away last night. I'd made my bed. I hadn't left my schoolwork on the kitchen table. I definitely hadn't sneaked any snacks. I was totally innocent. But there was no need to wonder—she'd tell me what it was soon enough.

15

It's a Wrap

I went to get your pills so I could renew your prescription." Mom held up a half-full pill bottle.

Uh-oh. I'd stopped taking my asthma medicine. I didn't need my inhaler. And I definitely didn't need my pills. I was supposed to take one every night. But a kid who doesn't breathe can't have an asthma attack. "I guess I forgot. I've been feeling real good. I've been jogging and everything."

I thought she was going to get angry. Instead, she nodded and said, "I understand. You're feeling good. But you can't take risks. That's how asthma is. The medicine builds up in your body over time. If you stop, you could have a bad attack." She held out the bottle.

"I'm sorry. I'll do better." I took the bottle. I realized I'd have to keep taking the pills. Except I wasn't going to swallow them. Nothing got digested anyhow. I didn't want to end up with a belly full of pills. But I had to swallow one, because Mom handed me a glass of water, then stood there and waited for me to do it. I figured one little pill in my stomach wouldn't be a problem.

Right after dinner, the doorbell rang. It was Abigail and Mookie.

"I figured something out," she said. "Can we come in?"

"Sure. Let's go up to my room."

When we got up there, Abigail said, "I have a theory. You always stink a little, right."

"Yeah. Thanks for reminding me."

"But sometimes it seems like you stink a lot." She grabbed my hand and sniffed it. "There's just a little smell right now. Do you see what that means?"

I took a guess. "Something makes me stinkier?"

Abigail gave me the same smile my teachers use when I come up with the right answer. "Exactly. So there's a trigger of some sort. Think about the times when you really stank."

"Every time he played sports before he became a zombie," Mookie said. "Nathan totally stank."

Abigail ignored him. "At lunch, when you handed Adam his burger, and in my room, when you picked up Mr. Fangle. When else?"

I thought back over the past week. I'd been smelly at home, right after I found out my show was canceled, and in the park with Mr. Murphy after he set off the sparks in my house. In the cafeteria, I'd been complaining about our table. And on the way to Abigail's room, I'd been annoyed with Mookie and his imaginary light saber.

I snapped my fingers. Carefully. "Got it. It happens when I'm angry."

"Perfect explanation," Abigail said. "Everything fits. Let's test it out. Your breath stinks, your nose is too big, and everybody hates you."

Those words sounded familiar. "That's exactly what you said back in your uncle's lab when we were trying to see if the Hurt-Be-Gone worked." I wasn't angry, because none of it was true. Though I guess my breath would start to stink pretty soon, along with the rest of me.

"Right, the lab," Abigail said. "It was really stupid of you to let yourself get splashed like that. You deserved what happened."

"Stupid? Hey, I didn't do anything except stand there! It was Mookie who tripped and splashed me.

Don't call me stupid. Your uncle is stupid. It's all his fault. He's—" I stopped my ranting when I noticed that Abigail was smiling. Then she sniffed. I sniffed, too.

"Phew," I said.

"Hypothesis proved," she said. "Anger makes you stinkier. Probably other strong emotions would, too."

"Hey, you're like the Incredible Hulk," Mookie said. "Except you're the Incredible Skunk. Or the Incredible Stink. Wait—even better. The Incredible Stunk. Cool. You're finally a superhero. But stink-on-demand is kind of my specialty, so you're going to have to make me your sidekick."

"Sure. Whatever." I sat down and slumped my head. "This is getting worse and worse." Not only did I stink— I couldn't even get angry about it.

"No, it's not worse. It's better," Abigail said. "It means that, at some level, your body is functioning. I'm not sure exactly what's going on, but if anger causes a change in you, you have some sort of metabolism. You're a bit more alive than we thought. I need to call Dr. Cushing right away. This is definitely encouraging."

"Will it help keep me from stinking?" I asked.

"At this point, I really don't know," Abigail said. She pulled out her cell phone and called Dr. Cushing. I listened while she talked, but as usual, didn't have much of a clue what they were talking about.

After Abigail and Mookie left, I made a decision. While I waited for someone to find a real cure for my stinkiness, I'd at least try out the quick fix Professor Quirlian offered.

That night, when I met up with Mr. Murphy, I told him my decision. "That's the spirit," he said. "Take advantage of what we have to offer. BUM looks out for its own. You won't be sorry."

He led me right down to the lab.

"Let's do it," I told Professor Quirlian.

"Super!" he said. "Come. All ready." He scurried to the other end of the lab and pointed to a door. "In there."

I opened the door. There was a tile wall like they had in the shower room at the YMCA. I saw a nozzle on the wall and, just past it, some sort of vent.

"Stand, close your eyes, turn slowly, count to twenty," Professor Quirlian said. "Then again, at the vent."

He closed the door. I stood there for a moment and talked to myself. "Okay. There's nothing here that can explode. It should be fine. It won't stop me from rotting, but at least it will keep me from stinking."

I took off my clothes, walked over to the nozzle, and closed my eyes. I heard a hiss like water was spraying on me. I turned and started counting. When I reached twenty, I made sure my back was to the nozzle and opened my eyes. I looked at my right hand. It was almost impossible to see the coating. If I looked hard, I could just catch a tiny shimmer.

I walked over to the vent. Air shot out. I turned and counted.

After I put my clothes on, Professor Quirlian came back in.

"Perfect!" he said.

"Thanks." I sniffed my hand. Nothing. Not even any kind of plastic smell. "This is great."

He reached out and patted my shoulder. "Trust science."

"I'll try."

I headed out of the room and left the lab. *I'm wrapped in plastic.* I sort of felt like a piece of meat in the supermarket display case. I hoped I hadn't made a bad decision.

I had another problem to deal with. Tomorrow was Friday. Which meant gym class—and the football game. I was pretty sure I'd figured out a way to keep from getting smashed by Ridley, but I wasn't looking forward to trying it.

16

Shredded Threads

When I left my house the next morning, I walked over to Spanky and held out my hand. He sniffed it once, then looked up at me like he was hoping for something else.

"Sorry," I said. "You'll have to find another dead kid to sniff."

This was good. If a dog couldn't smell me, I was definitely not going to stink around humans.

"I have great news," I said when I got to school.

"Not as great as mine," Mookie said.

"Of course not. It never is," I said. "What's your news?"

"My mom won two tickets to a cruise. It's a Midnight

Mystery Adventure Cruise for tomorrow night. She can't go, because she gets seasick. And Dad isn't supposed to leave the state. So she said I can go and take a friend."

"I have to keep available for a BUM mission tomorrow night." I didn't feel bad about that. A free cruise might sound pretty awesome, but nothing that Mookie's mom wins ever turns out to be as good as it sounds. Mookie's flashing sneakers reminded me of that.

"I love mysteries and adventure," Abigail said. "Besides, Mars and Jupiter will be in alignment. It would be amazing to see it from out on the ocean. I'll bring my binoculars."

"Great," Mookie said. "My mom asked my cousin to drive us there. It's just over at the docks in Perth Amboy."

"What's your news?" Abigail asked.

I told her about the coating Professor Quirlian had put on me. "It doesn't seem to be a problem. Do you see any danger?"

She thought for a moment, then said, "No. Nothing immediate. If it contains the smell, that would be good. Except . . ."

"Except what? Am I going to explode?"

"No. Nothing like that. It's just, odors are produced by gases. You don't want to let too much build up."

"I'll say." Mookie grinned at us. "That's why I always let the gas out before the pressure builds up."

"Don't get too angry, and you should be fine," Abigail said. "It's probably best to avoid any strong emotion—anger, fear. Speaking of fear, have you figured out what you're going to do about gym class?"

"Yeah. I know exactly what to do. I can't tell my mom I'm sick, but I can tell Mr. Lomux. I'll just get sick right at the start of gym class."

"He's not going to like it," Mookie said. "He still thinks you're some sort of champion."

"I'll deal with it," I said. I figured he wouldn't take the news well. That was actually okay. If I disappointed Mr. Lomux, he might stop paying so much attention to me. Attention is the last thing a dead kid wants. I guess that's another reason I liked being a spy. I could do my work in the shadows.

About five minutes after school started, there was an announcement over the loudspeaker from Mr. Tardis, the Borloff principal. It was just two sentences long.

"All classes to the cafetorium. Now."

"Whoa, he doesn't sound happy," I said. Usually, Mr. Tardis gave students an inspiring quote in the morning, about smiling or helping others.

"I wonder what I did this time," Mookie said.

We followed our teachers down the hall.

After we'd all wedged into the cafetorium, Mr. Tardis walked up to the microphone. "Something despicable has happened," he said. "Something worse than anything I've ever seen in my thirty-year career in education."

I looked at Mookie. He looked back, shrugged, and said, "For once, I don't think it's something I did."

"Probably not," I said. Mookie got in a lot of trouble, but it was never really bad stuff.

Principal Tardis walked to the very edge of the stage. "Mrs. Matheson and her wonderful kindergarten children were looking forward to marching in the parade. Their parents were looking forward to watching the parade. I know our eighth-grade guests were looking forward to their special role this year. And then a terrible person had to do this."

He held up something. I couldn't tell what it was. It looked like a torn fishing net.

"This," Principal Tardis said, "was once a wonderful animal costume, lovingly made by the parents of one of our sweet, innocent kindergartners. But her costume, along with every single other one, was destroyed last night by vandals."

"I knew this was going to end badly," Abigail said.

I remembered she'd said that when Mrs. Matheson first told us about the festival.

Principal Tardis stopped talking and stared out at us. I heard a snicker from behind me. A small one, but it was definitely a snicker. I looked back. Ridley was there, several rows away, fighting to keep a grin off his face.

So that's what this was about. Ridley, and maybe some of his friends, had trashed the costumes because they didn't want to stand there with little kids dressed as forest animals. I wanted to get up and shout in his face. I wanted to point at him and say, *He did it! He's the one.*

But I didn't have any proof. Even so, it definitely stank that he'd done this. I might be rotting. My skin might be starting to stink. But I was nowhere near as rotten as Ridley Mullasco.

He looked in my direction, grinned, pointed at me, and made a snapping motion with his fists, like he was breaking a stick. I shook my head, pointed back, and made the same motion. Somehow, I was going to break him.

The principal held up another mangled piece of cloth. This one was black with a white stripe. "Someone has broken a lot of little hearts."

"Man, this makes me angry," I said.

"No," Abigail said. "You can't let that happen."

"It's okay. I'm sealed in. Nobody will smell anything." I held up my hand and sniffed my fingers.

"Uh-oh . . . ," Abigail said.

"What?"

She pointed to the back of my hand. "You're getting blisters."

I looked. There were tiny bubbles in the coating. "How come?"

"Gas from the bacteria," she said. "Nothing to worry about right now. It doesn't look like much of a buildup."

She was right. The blisters were no bigger than pin-heads. It wouldn't be a problem. I turned my thoughts back to imagining horrible things happening to Ridley.

17

Instinct

When it was time for gym, I walked over to Mr. Lomux and said, "I feel sick." I clutched my stomach and tried to look like I was about to die. That's actually not all that hard when you're already dead. Just to make it more believable, I added, "I just came from lunch. I think the tuna fish was bad."

"Tough it out," he said.

"I'm really not feeling good," I said.

Mr. Scotus walked over. "What's the problem?"

"He says he's sick," Mr. Lomux said.

"Wimp!" Mr. Scotus shouted, getting right in my face. "Trying to weasel out of an honest game. You aren't sick.

I'll tell you who's sick. Me. Because little losers like you make me sick!"

He kept shouting at me. I backed away, feeling really glad I didn't need to breathe. I had a feeling his breath would make bad tuna seem like perfume. He moved closer and kept shouting.

"Pathetic little whiner!" He seemed just as likely as Ridley to start breaking me into pieces. I couldn't believe they let people like him work around kids all day.

I tried to move away, but I'd backed into the wall. Something weird was happening. My whole body felt like it was being squeezed. I don't feel pain, but I can feel pressure. I glanced down at my hands. The plastic was puffing up. My fingers looked like they belonged to a cartoon character.

"Look at me when I'm talking to you!" Mr. Scotus shouted.

I tried to keep my eyes aimed in his direction. But I could feel the plastic inflating all around me. I risked a glance at my chest. It was swelling.

"You," he said, poking me in the chest.

"—aren't—" He poked me again.

"—getting—"

Poke.

"—out—"

Poke.

"—of—"

Poke.

I guess the next word would have been *gym*. Or maybe *class*. I'll never know. Instead of a word, I heard a loud pop, followed by a hiss. He'd broken the plastic and released all the stink that had built up under the coating.

But both Mr. Lomux and Mr. Scotus gasped—I guess because of what they'd sniffed. Gasping was a mistake. That gave them an even bigger whiff, filling their noses and lungs with rotten air.

Their bodies jerked. Oh, man—I'd seen that before, and knew what was coming. I was about to get splattered. That was fine. It would get me out of gym. But they both spun away from me as they hurled. Too bad for them—they spun right toward each other.

They looked like those rotating lawn sprinklers that throw a curved stream of water. Each of them hit the other with an impressive spray. They both staggered back, then fell to the ground.

Wow. I looked down at my shirt. It was spotless. I hadn't gotten a drop on me. I guess someone called the nurse. She came and almost threw up when she saw what was there. But she got under control quickly and started to lead them off. By the time the Borloff gym teacher showed up to take over the class, it was too late to play football.

Ridley walked up to me. "Monday," he said. He pointed at me, and then Mookie. "Both of you." He made that snapping motion again. I decided this wasn't a good time for a smart comment. He was already frustrated. If I pushed him, he'd start a fight, no matter what the principal had threatened. So I kept my mouth shut.

"Skunk!" Abigail shouted when I met up with her after school.

"Ha, ha, very funny," I said. "I thought you'd be the last person to insult me."

"No, I mean that's our temporary solution," she said. "Remember the place my mom and I were staying before we moved to our new house?"

"Sure," I said. "The Comfy Craven Motel and Bait Shop. What about it?"

"I used to go for a walk every night. I'm pretty sure I saw a skunk in the field behind the place."

"So?" I wasn't sure I liked where this was going.

"So we get you sprayed," she said. "The odor will cover anything. By the time the stink fades away, I'm sure we'll have a permanent solution. And the smell won't even really be on your skin, since you're still coated with that plastic. You can actually peel it off if you want to."

"And meanwhile, I'll smell like a skunk?"

Abigail nodded. "But that's perfect. It won't bother you, since you don't need to breathe."

"And it will be kind of cool," Mookie said. "I mean, you hear about it happening, and you see it in the movies. But I don't know any kid who's ever actually been sprayed by a skunk. You'd be the first in our school. They might even put your picture on the wall."

"I think I've had enough firsts," I said.

"If you stink badly enough," Abigail said, "your parents might let you stay home from school on Monday. So, no football."

"No football . . ." That sounded good. And no rotting smell. Maybe it would be sort of cool to get skunked. Mookie was right. I'd heard about it happening, and seen it in the movies, but didn't know anyone who'd actually been sprayed. "Okay. I'll try it."

So we headed to the field behind the motel.

"Skunks generally avoid people," Abigail said when we got there. "And they won't use their spray unless they feel really threatened. So, Nathan, you stand in the middle of the field. Mookie and I will walk around the edge. The skunk will run away from us. When it gets near you, just jump up and down, wave your arms, and shout at it. That should scare it into spraying you."

"You're sure about this?" I asked.

Abigail gave me a confident smile. "What could go wrong?"

When had I heard that before? But it was usually from Mookie, not Abigail, so I wasn't worried.

I headed toward the middle of the field. "Let's split up," Abigail told Mookie. "That way, we can cover twice as much of the perimeter at the same time."

She walked to the other side of the field, then waved at Mookie. They started walking along the edge of the field. I waited. At one point, Abigail froze. Then she pointed at the ground. I saw something running toward me through the tall grass. It was black with two white stripes. No mistake. I was about to get skunked.

Here goes.

When the skunk got close, I jumped up, came down facing right at it, waved my arms, and screamed, "Bugga bugga! Whoooo! Yahhhh! Yibba-yibba-yibba!"

The skunk didn't even slow down. It ran between my legs and kept going—right toward Mookie. When it got close to him, it finally stopped. Mookie stared at the skunk. The skunk stared at Mookie. Mookie let out a fart I could hear all the way over in the middle of the field. For once, he was outgunned. The skunk turned and fired a shot of spray.

It hit Mookie right in the chest.

"Gaahhhhhh!" Mookie spun away from the skunk and ran toward the motel.

Abigail and I followed him.

"I guess it didn't think I was alive," I said.

"What?" Abigail asked.

"Animals don't react to me like I'm living," I said.

"And you just decided to mention this?"

I could still hear screams from the other side of the motel. They were followed by a large splash.

"Yeah. I suppose I should have told you earlier."

"It's not your fault," Abigail said. "I should have realized there might be a problem. Now that I know about it, it does make sense."

We'd reached the motel pool, which was closed but still had water in it. Green water loaded with bugs and leaves. Mookie had jumped in and was thrashing around like an injured rhino.

"How long will he stink?" I asked.

"All his life," Abigail said, "unless he changes his eating habits."

"I mean, from the skunk."

"Couple days," Abigail said. "Maybe a week."

"He's used to it," I said.

Abigail took a bottle of lotion from her purse and rubbed some on her hands. "Better him than me," she said.

"I guess so."

She held out the bottle. "Want some? It's strawberry-kiwi."

"No thanks." I wasn't adding any more smells to my body right now. And I was peeling off the plastic as soon as I got home. I didn't want to build up another stink bomb.

18

Cruising Around

Nathan, **remember when** we worked on drops?" Mr. Murphy asked when we got together that night behind Belgosi Upper Elementary.

"Sure. On the playground. I practice every time I throw something in the trash or mail a letter. Why'd you ask about that?"

"Sometimes the bad guys make a drop. If we know about it, we can intercept the package. We believe there's a drop happening tomorrow night. It's a perfect mission for you. Be prepared."

"What are they dropping?" I asked.

"You don't need to know," he said.

"Look, I'm not buying that stuff anymore." I jabbed my thumb against my chest. "I'm the kid who had the misadventure, right?"

He nodded.

"And you're with the Bureau of Useful Misadventures. Right?"

He nodded again.

"So I'm what this whole place is about. I'm the most important person. The more I know, the better chance I have to do what you ask me to do. Right?"

"Perhaps."

"Then tell me what's being dropped," I said.

He shrugged. "I can't. We don't know."

"You don't know? Why didn't you just tell me that in the first place?"

"Because you didn't need to know."

I swirled that around in my brain for a moment, then kicked it back out. "Do you see how crazy that sounds? You didn't tell me that you didn't know, because you felt I didn't need to know that you didn't know."

"When you put it that way, it does sound a bit convoluted."

"Does that mean 'twisty'?"

He nodded.

"Do you at least know who's making the drop?" I asked.

I expected him to tell me I didn't need to know. I was surprised when he said, "RABID."

"Them again." That was the group that had kidnapped Mr. Murphy. They were pretty evil.

"The files you captured led us to other information that led to still other items. One of the benefits of all this is we learned an item was being transferred by drop tomorrow night. Now you know everything that I know. Meet me at headquarters as soon as you can tomorrow evening."

I hung out with Mookie and Abigail at her place on Saturday afternoon. Abigail's mom asked us to play outside, since Mookie skunked up the indoors pretty quickly. Mookie's mom had washed him down with tomato juice, like everyone says you're supposed to do, but it didn't help all that much. Right now, he was running around, pretending to be Captain Stink Bomb.

Abigail was excited about the cruise. "My mom was worried at first, since no parents would be on the ship with us. But she called the cruise company, and they told her kids come on their cruises all the time. The crew keeps an eye on them. Not that we need to be watched. It's going to be a wonderful experience."

I pointed to Mookie's flashing sneakers as he ran past

us, and whispered, "That's what the cruise will be like. One way or another, it won't be as good as it sounds."

"I don't care," she said. "I love the ocean. And the forecast is for clear skies." She grabbed her binoculars. "It will be perfect conditions for observation."

I hoped she enjoyed herself. And I figured Mookie would have a good time, since he seemed to be happy no matter what he was doing. I guess he was sort of lucky in a way. I couldn't imagine even wearing those sneakers, let alone being thrilled about them.

I hung out with my friends until dinnertime. It wasn't much fun at home. Mom didn't even want to talk. The bear thing had really been hard on her. She hadn't messed up everything, so the store had some new things for the big day. But Mom was definitely hurting.

I wished I could use my zombie skills to help her out. But at least, I could use them that night. After I went to BUM, Mr. Murphy took me to another of the elevators. This one brought us to the headquarters for the East Coast branch of the Pollen Collectors' Meeting Room in Staten Island.

"We don't have far to go," Mr. Murphy said as he led me to a car near the curb. "The drop is at a pier."

"What's there that needs my skills?" I asked.

"Guard dogs."

"No problem." I was glad I didn't have to climb an

electric fence or sneak into a sewer plant. This one would be easy.

We drove south for a while, and then swung into a shipping area with a bunch of factories and stuff near the water. Mr. Murphy parked and led me toward a pier. We stopped next to one of those large cranes they use to load giant cargo boxes onto ships.

"Here it is," he whispered, pointing ahead of us. "Number Thirty-seven. I can't go any closer. The dogs will start barking. You'll be fine. Just go to the ship and find the package. This will help locate it. The nearer you get, the brighter the lights will flash." He handed me a flat object the size of a calculator, with a display window.

"Is this going to explode?" I asked.

"Nathan, will you ever stop asking that?"

"Well, will it?"

"Of course not," Mr. Murphy said. "It's just a simple tracker, right from the electronics store."

I looked toward the end of the pier. There was a locked gate. I could see dark forms pacing around, like wolves. Beyond that, something bobbed in the water. As Abigail had said, it would be a clear night. Under the light of the stars and half moon, I stared at the bobbing shape.

"Is that what I think it is?" I asked.

"Afraid so." Mr. Murphy chuckled, then said, "That wasn't part of our information. But it shouldn't be a problem for you."

"No, it shouldn't." I still didn't like it. But this was no time for complaints. Hoping the mission wouldn't be as messy as it looked, but knowing it would probably end up being even messier, I climbed the fence.

19

Barging In

I slipped down the other side of the fence. Like before, the dogs ran toward me, then lost interest. I walked past them toward the ship. Except, as I'd seen from the other side, it wasn't a ship. It was a barge or something. Just a flat boat with two giant heaps of garbage on it.

"Yay," I muttered. At least it wasn't sewage.

The barge bobbed beneath my feet as I walked onto it. It was tied to a post on the dock. I watched the rope pull tight each time the barge bobbed. The rope looked sort of frayed. I went over to check it out. Way past the fence, I saw Mr. Murphy waving at me to get going.

I realized I was just stalling because I didn't feel like facing mountains of garbage. At least I had a tracker. I didn't see any signal on it yet. There was room around the sides to walk past the garbage. I circled the heaps, watching the signal on the tracker. The light finally blinked on when I was near the second heap.

Okay. Now I just had to get an idea what part of the heap had the package. The mound rose about ten feet over my head, but it wasn't too steep. I started to climb up to the top. It was pretty squishy. Sort of like walking on a combination of mud and mattresses. Most of the garbage was in plastic bags. But most of the bags had split open.

The signal seemed strongest about halfway to the top of the heap. Then it started getting weaker. I'd played several computer games that used trackers like this, so I knew exactly what to do. I went partway around the mound and climbed it again. Yup. Same results. The light was strongest halfway up. The drop was right in the middle of the heap.

Mookie's cruise would be better than this. I wouldn't mind being out at sea right now with him. Even if it was on some sort of trip that would turn out not to be any fun.

I shot a glare toward the pier, aiming right where Mr. Murphy was probably standing. I could just hear his silly little laugh as he watched me crawl into the middle of a pile of garbage.

No point stalling any longer.

I headed in. It was sort of like I was a giant earthworm. I crawled, wriggled, clawed, and even sort of swam as I made my way deeper. I could feel the barge rocking and shifting.

Finally, with the help of the signal, I reached something that felt like a small briefcase, maybe six or eight inches wide. Now I had to get out of the mound. I figured it would be easier to just keep crawling toward the other side rather than trying to back out.

I don't know how long it took. But finally, I popped out of the mound and slid back down to the deck of the barge. Great. I was done. Except for burning my clothes and taking a really long shower.

Whoa. I almost lost my balance as the barge rocked hard. I looked toward the pier.

"What?"

All I saw around me was water.

I ran to the back of the barge. The tie-up rope dangled in the water, floating behind the barge as we drifted.

It had broken loose.

Great. I was out in the ocean on a barge piled with garbage.

I saw something glitter in the moonlight. Water lapped at my feet.

Double great. I was out in the ocean on a sinking barge piled with garbage.

I got out my cell phone. The signal was really weak. I wasn't sure who to call. I didn't even have a number for Mr. Murphy. I called Abigail. I just hoped she wasn't too far from land either. Luckily, she answered.

"I think I'm in trouble," I told her. "I'm on some sort of garbage boat. It's drifting. I think it's also sinking."

"Is it a big flat barge with two heaps of garbage on it?" Abigail asked. "Sort of like a double-scoop banana split?"

"How do you know?" I asked.

"I can see it. I brought my binoculars. You're just a hundred yards away from us, but you're drifting farther. There's a life raft back here. Mookie and I can take it and come get you. They crammed way too many people on the boat. It's been an awful trip. The only mystery is that they don't seem to know where they're going. Nobody will miss us. Everyone is avoiding us because Mookie stinks, so we should be able to slip away."

"That sounds dangerous," I said. "Maybe I can swim to your boat."

"We're moving too quickly. You'd never catch us. There's no time to discuss this. We have to do it now before you get too far away."

"I don't think that's a good idea."

The connection went dead. She'd hung up on me. I walked around the edge of the barge and scanned the ocean until I spotted the ship. It wasn't too far away, but I couldn't see any raft. I watched and waited until the ship shrank to nothing in the distance.

I hoped they were coming. The water on the barge was already up to my ankles. The whole thing was starting to tilt. I spotted a faint flashing light. Soon after that, I saw the raft. Mookie and Abigail were both rowing.

I think it was the only time I'd seen them working together on something. Well, sort of together. The raft would move toward me for a while, then start to go sideways. The two of them would yell at each other and get things straightened out. I saw brighter flashes as they got closer. Mookie had worn his new sneakers.

"Man, am I glad to see you," I said when they reached the barge. I unhitched my belt, put the end through the handle of the briefcase, then made sure it was fastened. I wasn't going to go through all of this and not deliver the package. "This thing is sinking."

"I'll help you in," Mookie said. He stood up in the raft.

"That's okay. I can do it." I put one foot in the raft.

"No, let me help." Mookie reached for me. The raft rocked. I grabbed his hand. He pulled. I fell into the raft. Mookie caught his foot under one of the oars and toppled forward.

But for once, it looked like we'd ended up okay. I was in the raft and off the sinking barge. Safe and dry. Now all we had to do was row to shore.

I heard a rude noise. *Brrffffttttt.*

"Mookie!" I shouted. "Can't you ever hold anything in?"

He was still facedown. He rolled over and frowned. "That wasn't me."

We looked at Abigail. "Hey!" she shouted. "Don't even think it. I'd never make that kind of noise."

We heard a louder one. *Phrtt burble blooooopphhhh.*

"That sounded really wet," Mookie said. "Uh-oh . . ." He glanced back toward his feet.

So did I.

His sneakers were jammed against the bottom of the raft. I didn't see anything flashing. He rolled over. The bulbs in his toes had been broken when he fell.

Jagged pieces of glass stuck out of the bottom of the raft. Water seeped in through the gashes.

"We're sinking!" Mookie screamed. "Mayday! SOS! Help!"

"We're okay," Abigail said. "Life rafts always have several compartments, each of which can keep it afloat. It's the law. We might get wet, but we won't sink."

Mookie leaned over and read a label on the side of the raft next to him. "Manufactured by Squinky Novelty Company, Brumigan, Illinois. Not for use as a flotation device."

"Great," Abigail said. "It's some kind of toy." She glared toward the direction of the cruise ship. "Cheapskates!"

Two minutes later, the raft was totally sunk. Mookie and Abigail were treading water on either side of me. Above us, the stars were out. It would have been a beautiful night if we weren't stranded at sea.

"This is bad," Abigail said. "We're probably at least three or four miles from shore. The water is too cold for us to swim very far."

"BUM will search for us," I said. "They'll call the coast guard and everything."

"We'll be easy to find," Mookie said. "We're probably the only people floating out here right now."

"Needle in a haystack," Abigail said. "The ocean is huge. They don't know where we are." She sank under a swell, popped back up, and started coughing.

"Save your breath," I said. "We can make it."

Abigail shook her head. "I wish you were right. But the odds against rescue are enormous."

"Then we have to rescue ourselves," I said.

"How?" Abigail asked. "It's too far to swim."

"Not for me." I didn't get tired. The cold water wouldn't bother me either. I could swim for hours if I had to. And I could pull them with me. "Which way is land?"

Abigail looked up at the stars, then pointed past my left shoulder. "That way. Just head toward those three stars."

"I'll float, you two hang on."

"Take a deep breath first," Abigail said.

"I don't need air," I told her.

"Fill your lungs," she said. "It will help you float."

I knew what she meant. I used to like to float on my back in the town pool. When I took in a breath, I'd rise. When I let it out, I'd sink a bit. I started to float on my back, but I realized I could swim better if I was on my stomach.

"Grab my legs," I said. I took a big breath, closed my lips, then tilted forward and floated on my stomach. I waited until Mookie and Abigail grabbed my legs. Then I started swimming.

I could feel them dragging me, but it didn't matter. I could swim as far as I needed. I could keep going until I reached the shore.

But I stopped before then. Something great happened. While I was swimming, I started thinking. I had plenty of time to do that. I thought about how Abigail was always seeing the way that things were connected, and always finding answers. And I thought about my problems. Not the being-dead thing. I'd need her help and lots of other help with that.

But I thought about Ridley. And about other stuff in my life. And I saw a pattern in how Ridley acted. And the pattern gave me a clue about how I could survive the football game on Monday. It was exciting enough of an idea that I wanted to get Abigail thinking about it, too.

I stopped swimming and rolled over on my back.

"Are we there yet?" Mookie asked.

"Nope. How are you two doing?" I asked.

"Fine," Abigail said. "Cold. But I'll survive."

"I'm pretending I'm a torpedo," Mookie said. "I've sunk three enemy boats so far."

"Listen, I have an idea I want you to think about. I'll need your help." I told them and then went back to swimming.

We finally reached land, not far from the pier I'd left. I found a low dock and we scrambled up out of the water. We walked over to the crane. Mr. Murphy was there. A bunch of other people had showed up, along with several cars and a trailer.

I glanced from Mr. Murphy to my friends and back.

"I found them at sea," I said. "They fell off a cruise ship."

"And now you want to keep them?" he asked.

"What?"

"Nathan, you're very clever, and you have wonderful spy instincts, but you can't fool me." He pointed right at Mookie. "I've known about your friends since well before that little stink bomb factory over there fouled the air in Dr. Cushing's car."

He led us to the trailer. About twenty minutes later, someone showed up with dry clothes for all of us. Then we got in one of the cars, and Mr. Murphy drove Mookie and Abigail back to the dock area for the mystery cruise, where Mookie's cousin was going to pick them up. The ship was just pulling in, so Mookie and Abigail could mingle with the crowd and pretend they just came off.

"I'll call you tomorrow," I said as my friends got out of the car.

"That was awesome," Mookie said when they walked off.

"Awesome?" Abigail said.

They started arguing. I stopped listening.

"I'm sorry the briefcase got wet," I said as we drove off.

"Wet isn't a problem," Mr. Murphy said. "I'm sorry I couldn't do anything when the barge broke loose."

"I survived," I said.

"I never doubted you would."

"So, what's in there?" I asked.

He opened his mouth. I guess he was going to tell me I didn't need to know. But he paused, looked at his watch, then said, "The night is still young, lad. Why don't you come back to BUM and we can look through it together. Sound good?"

"Sounds great."

20

What's Bugging Him?

I only got through about half the documents that night before it was time to go home. Some of it was interesting, but a lot of it was boring. I guess that's how it was in the spy world. But I could tell from Mr. Murphy's reaction that most of it was important.

There was also a wad of money in the briefcase, for another of RABID's evil plans. So we'd probably saved a lot more people. I wasn't keeping score, but it looked like I was definitely helping to make the world a better place.

Now I had just one more small bit of evil to deal

with. If I succeeded, I'd be making a lot of kids happier, and safer—which was also a way to make the world a better place.

I met up with Abigail and Mookie right after breakfast on Sunday. Luckily, Mom had taken a day off from work, even though it was Bear Season.

"I need you to do this." I handed Abigail the money I'd won at the oyster-eating contest. "I can't take a chance that they'd recognize me."

"Some spy you are," she said. "Can't you come up with a decent disguise?"

Before I could say anything, she laughed and said, "I'm kidding. I'll be happy to do it. It's for a good cause. Two good causes, if we're right. And when have we ever been wrong?"

"You sure you don't want me to do it?" Mookie asked.

"No way. You'd probably come back with five hundred dollars' worth of candy."

"They don't sell candy in there," he said.

"You'd still find a way to buy some," I said.

Mookie shrugged. "You're right. I have a gift for that. It's amazing the places you can find candy. Even the pet store has it."

"I don't want to hear the rest of this," Abigail said. She went into Stuffy Wuffy with my prize money.

She was gone for at least twenty minutes. But when

she came back, she smiled and said, "We're all set. They'll deliver everything right away."

"Great. I really hope this works." No matter what, Mom would feel better when she found out. And she'd never know it was because of me. That was good. I'd set my plan in motion. But we still had a lot of work to do.

I had to wait until the next morning to find out if I'd been right. The first part went just the way I'd hoped. About an hour after school started, we were called down for an assembly. This time, Principal Tardis sounded happy.

I smiled at Abigail. She winked and nodded.

After everyone filed into the cafetorium, Mrs. Matheson went to the stage and picked up the microphone. "Eighth-graders," she said. She clapped her hands like she was giving orders to a show dog. The eighth-graders got up, groaning, and walked toward the stage.

"This is going to be awesome," I said to Mookie.

"I wish I had a camera," he said.

After all the eighth-graders had gotten to the stage, Mrs. Matheson said, "We had feared the animal parade wouldn't happen this year. As you know, the costumes were destroyed. But then something amazing happened."

I sneaked a peek at Ridley's face. He didn't seem to have any clue what was going on.

"We received a donation," Mrs. Matheson said. "Someone who wishes to remain anonymous gave us costumes. Wonderful costumes. Enough for every child."

She turned toward the side of the stage and clapped her hands again. The kindergartners streamed out. Dozens of them.

"Boys and girls," Mrs. Matheson said, "I am thrilled to introduce the March of the Happy Insects."

The kids, dressed in the outfits I'd bought from Stuffy Wuffy, swarmed onto the stage. With the help of Abigail's mom, who was good at sewing, we'd stuffed the arms and legs of the pajamas and then cut extra armholes in the sides of each, below the stuffed arms. We also cut new legholes at the bottom. We'd stitched on the wings in back and glued two of the giant gems onto each hood.

The costumes turned each kindergartner into a giant fly. A cute giant fly, but with the six limbs—plus their real legs—wings, and faceted eyes, definitely a fly.

I watched, hoping I was right about Ridley.

"Aggghhhh!"

He let out a scream so loud, you'd think someone was trying to remove his appendix with a Popsicle stick. His face grew pale. He backed away from the bugs, but they closed around him, making buzzing sounds.

"Hey—it looks like even big flies are attracted to garbage," I said.

Ridley screamed louder and leaped from the stage. He turned and shot across the room, crashing through a door that led to the outside. He kept running until he was nothing but a small dot, and then nothing at all.

It felt good to be right. He'd reacted when Abigail mentioned a bee. And unlike Rodney, who had good reason to fear vomit, Ridley fled from the puke because of the insects. I guess the final clue was in gym class when Mr. Lomux and Mr. Scotus both got sick. I realized that hadn't bothered Ridley at all. He wasn't afraid of vomit—he was afraid of insects. Luckily, it looked like he was especially afraid of big insects.

"Think he'll miss gym?" Mookie asked.

"Most likely," I said. "I don't think he's going to stop running for a while."

I looked back at the stage. The rest of the eighth-graders seemed to be happy being with the kindergartners. And the little kids were definitely thrilled.

"Nice save," Abigail said.

"Thanks."

She laughed. "It gives a whole new meaning to *debugging*."

We sat and watched the happy insects as they marched around the room. It was fun.

"Hey," Abigail said at the end of the assembly, "hold up your hand."

"Why?"

"I don't smell anything," she said.

"I'm not angry right now," I said.

"It doesn't matter," she said. "You'd started smelling a little bit all the time. But not now."

I held out my hand.

She sniffed it cautiously. Then she sniffed harder. "Definitely no smell," she said.

I took a sniff. She was right. "What happened?"

Abigail stared up at the ceiling for a moment. "Got it! Think where you've been where you don't normally go."

"Oh, a riddle. I love riddles," Mookie said. "Can you ask it again, but make it rhyme? That would be even more fun."

"It's not a riddle," Abigail said. "I'm just pointing Nathan to the solution."

I thought back. There was one obvious answer. "The ocean?"

"Yup," Abigail said. "Salt and bacteria don't get along. And salt is used to preserve meat. They make bacon by curing it in salt."

"So I was right!" Mookie said. "I told you salt could cure a zombie."

"That's a different type of cure," Abigail said. "But it still doesn't make complete sense. There's also bacteria inside you. Especially in your stomach. You didn't swallow any water when we were in the ocean, did you?"

"Not a drop."

"Mookie had you swallow some salt, but it wasn't enough to do anything. Did you eat anything at all recently?" she asked.

"The oysters," I said. "But I'd rather not ever think about that again."

"That can't be it. The bacteria would feast on them. Anything else?"

"Nope." I didn't eat at all these days. "Wait—Mom made me take my asthma medicine."

"What do you take?" Abigail asked.

I told her.

She nodded. "That's a new one. I'm pretty sure it has antibacterial side effects. That explains a lot. Did you stop taking it after you became a zombie?"

"Yeah. I didn't need it. How'd you know I'd stopped?"

"Because that helps explain the timing," Abigail said. "The medicine stayed in your body for a while after you stopped, because your metabolism is so slow. But it finally ran out—which is why you started to stink. Now we know you need to keep taking it."

"So I'm not cured," I said. "But at least I don't stink. Will it last?"

"The effect should last seven or eight days," Abigail said. "But that's good enough. Just rub some salt on yourself once a week when you shower. Or put some in a bath. And take your pill. It won't be a problem. It's small enough so your body will be able to slowly absorb it."

"Great. That'll be easy enough." I was still dead, but at least I wouldn't be making a stink about it.

Later

Ridley didn't make it back to school in time for gym class. We still got clobbered at football, but the eighth-graders weren't mean about it. Nobody got hurt. They played to win, but they didn't play for blood. I didn't have to bring out the glue. It was actually fun playing against them. The one time we scored a touchdown, it felt like a giant victory.

We were able to go back to our own school on Wednesday, so I'm totally safe from Ridley until next year, when I go to the middle school. By then, he would have forgotten about me. I think Ridley has the same kind of memory as Spanky, though I'm pretty sure Spanky is smarter. Even if Ridley doesn't forget about me, I'm sure Mr. Murphy will have taught me all sorts of spy-style self-defense by then. I need to ask him about that.

Stuffy Wuffy decided to expand its business and sell costumes for little kids. They opened a second shop just for that. They called it Stuffy Wuffy Dressy Uppy. Yeah. Gag me. They put Mom in charge of the whole thing. She was thrilled. She got to design the costumes. But she lets someone else place the orders on the computer. That was a smart move.

The only bad part is that nearly every day is part of Bear Season now. On the bright side, Dad and I have started jogging almost every evening.

The next time I saw Mr. Murphy, he showed me the rest of the papers I'd gotten from RABID. The information was interesting, but the part I liked the most was that he trusted me, and treated me like we were equals.

The salt and medicine are keeping me from stinking. But I know I have to do something more. My body is still rotting. I need to find a cure. I think I need to find it soon.

READ ON FOR A SNEAK PEEK OF

ENTER THE ZOMBIE

Nathan Abercrombie,
Accidental Zombie
— BOOK FIVE

"**This must be** serious," I said as Mookie, Abigail, and I left Belgosi Upper Elementary School.

"Unprecedented," Abigail said.

"He's not a president," Mookie said. "At least, I don't think he is. And if he was, he probably wouldn't tell anyone."

Abigail groaned, but didn't bother to say anything. I had a feeling I knew what *unprecedented* meant. This had never happened before, not counting the first time he'd approached me. But it was happening now. The master spy who had recruited me and trained me, the man who did everything in secret, was standing in public, right in front of the school, waiting for me. He wasn't even wearing any sort of disguise or hiding behind a large plant.

"We need to talk," Mr. Murphy said when I reached him.

I couldn't even begin to guess what this was about.

"We'll catch up with you," Abigail said. She tugged at Mookie's arm. "Come on. Let's leave them alone."

"Hold on. We *all* need to talk." Mr. Murphy tucked his little finger under his thumb, then aimed his other fingers in our direction. "The three of you. Right now. But let's not stand here where we'll attract attention."

He headed down the street. I stared at his back for a moment, then raced to catch up with him.

"Well, that definitely won't attract any attention," he said. "Would you like to hop and skip, too? Or is running enough? You could sing at the top of your lungs. That would be a nice touch. Maybe we can find you some sparklers to wave around."

I tried to think of some smart-alecky reply to throw back at him, but he was right. Spies should never attract attention—unless they're doing it on purpose to distract people from secret actions being done by other spies. "What's going on?"

"We have a chance to take out RABID from the very top," he said. "If we act now, we can cut the head off the snake. That would be a major step toward destroying them."

He definitely had my attention. I'd love to see RABID wiped out. The name stood for Raise Anarchy by Inciting Disorder. They wanted to control people by making them unhappy with their leaders. They were responsible for plenty of the bad things that happened in the world. They would have done even more bad things if Mr. Murphy and I hadn't been around to stop some of their plans.

"But you said they're too spread out to get rid of." From what I knew, RABID worked in little groups all around the world. Mr. Murphy called the groups *cells*.

"We think we know how to locate the man at the very top of the organization. If we can capture Baron von Lyssa, the cells won't survive for long." Mr. Murphy pulled a folded sheet of paper from his pocket and handed it to me. "Ever heard of this?"

I opened it up and read the first three lines.

MIND AND BODY
Enter a Team in the Ultimate
Athletic and Academic Competition!

Below the headline, there was a drawing of a kid with a big head and bulging muscles. He had a dumbbell in one hand and a book in the other. The flyer looked sort of familiar. "I saw this on the bulletin board last month," I said. It had quickly gotten covered by posters about the band concert, the bake sale, and all sorts of other stuff. "They put up an announcement every year. Nobody from our school ever enters."

I noticed Abigail was staring at the flyer. Then her gaze drifted toward the clouds, like she was thinking about something.

"That kid must have to buy his hats somewhere special," Mookie said. "What's that have to do with us, anyhow?"

"We think RABID looks for exceptional young people and convinces them to join the organization. Sometimes, they start working on their candidates when they're years away from becoming active."

"And kids who enter the contest are more likely to have the sorts of skills that RABID would find useful," Abigail said. "Especially the winners."

"I've been told you're quite smart," Mr. Murphy said. "Apparently, that's the case. I assume you know what I'm going to ask next."

"Ooohhh! Let me guess!" Mookie raised his hand, like we were in class, waved it wildly, and then shouted out, "You want us to parachute out of a jet and attack the bad guys. Right?" He clenched his fists above his shoulders, the way people do when they're hanging under a parachute. Then he tugged down with his left fist and skittered in that direction.

Mr. Murphy made a face like he'd just tried to swallow a large slice of moldy onion. "Well, lad, I wouldn't mind dropping you out of a jet, preferably over an empty stretch of ocean, but that's not exactly the current plan. Though I'll keep it in mind for later, should an opportunity arise."

"No jet?" Mookie asked.

"No jet," Mr. Murphy said.

"He wants us to form a team, enter the competition, and do well enough that we're approached by RABID," Abigail said. "That's why he's talking to all three of us. Each Mind and Body team has three people on it."

"That was my next guess," Mookie said. "But I didn't want to show off too much. Nobody likes a smarty-pants. Or a smarty-skirt."

"Correct, again." Mr. Murphy nodded at Abigail, who happened to be wearing a skirt today.

"Okay, so you want us to enter the contest," I said. "I guess we have a chance to do well. But why didn't you just send a message to me like you usually do?"

"There wasn't time. We figured out the connection between RABID and Mind and Body late this morning, right before the sign-up deadline. All three of you need

169

to fill out an entry form immediately." He handed each of us a sheet of paper and a pen. "Fill these out and I'll mail them right away. But before you do, I need to make sure all of you understand what you're getting into."

"A jet?" Mookie asked.

I had a good idea I knew what Mr. Murphy meant. "We'll be meeting with a very dangerous person. At some point, we might be on our own, out of touch with BUM. If we mess up, there won't be anyone to come to our rescue."

"Exactly," Mr. Murphy said. "Wherever you go to meet him, you'll be scanned for electronic devices, so we can't use any sort of tracker or beacon. You'll be isolated. They'll take steps to make sure you aren't being followed. We'll have no way to communicate. If they suspect you, bad things could happen. There are definite dangers. The choice is yours."

ABOUT THIS GUIDE: The information, activities, and discussion questions that follow are intended to enhance your reading of *The Big Stink*. Please feel free to adapt these materials to suit your needs and interests.

WRITING AND RESEARCH ACTIVITIES

I. Big and Small

A. At the start of the novel, Nathan and his friends find themselves sitting in a classroom meant for much smaller kids. Consider how Nathan, Abigail, and Mookie each react to the situation. Try riding a tricycle, wandering around a toddler playground, squeezing into an outgrown jacket, or exploring another object or place that is not sized for you. Write a poem or song lyrics describing your thoughts and feelings about this experience.

B. Watch a movie about changing size, such as *Honey, I Shrunk the Kids; Gulliver's Travels; The Incredible Shrinking Woman; Big;* or *Alice in Wonderland*. Write a review of the movie, commenting particularly on images and themes of growing larger or smaller. Use a quote from *The Big Stink* to lend insight to your review.

C. At Borloff Lower, Nathan observes older and younger kids getting along and coming into conflict. In groups, brainstorm ways to create a playground or lunchroom environment where kids of different ages can feel safe and have fun together. Have each group create an illustrated poster, PowerPoint, or other planned presentation for friends and classmates.

II. Winning and Losing

A. The notion of winning and losing can be found throughout the Nathan Abercrombie books, from Mookie's mom's constant prize winning to the various sports competitions Nathan encounters at school to BUM's battles to defeat RABID. Go to the library or online to find definitions of "win" and "lose." Write these words at opposite ends of a large sheet of paper. Add magazine clippings, photographs, drawings, small objects, and quotations to create a word collage depicting what winning and losing mean to you.

B. David Lubar describes many situations where Nathan and his friends seem like they are about to win, only to have them lose. For example, Abigail and Mookie come to rescue Nathan on the barge only to realize their lifeboat (a "win") is a useless toy (a "loss"). Make a list of moments in the story where this win-lose switch takes place. Discuss how this plotting technique works well in the novel.

C. Can you win and lose at the same time? Have you ever won something but felt like a loser—or lost a prize and felt like a winner? Are there moments in *The Big Stink* where the line between winning and losing isn't quite clear? With friends or classmates, make a reading list of other books, movies, plays, and songs that explore the idea of winning and losing. Make sure each student from the group contributes at least one entry along with a two-to-three sentence explanation of why their title belongs on the list.

D. With friends or classmates, role-play a conversation between Nathan and his teammates as they get into their football huddle to try to lose so they don't have to play the eighth-graders. Role-play a second huddle chat where the fifth-graders discuss changing strategies to try to win. (Hint: Don't worry about realistic football dialogue. Student-actors should discuss their strategies, reasons for trying to win or lose, and concerns about what will happen after the game.) Finally, role-play the conversation between the fifth-grade and eighth-grade players after the football game actually takes place at the end of the story.

III. Safe and Sorry

A. One feature of Nathan's zombie status is that animals, such as guard dogs and skunks, don't recognize him as alive, so they do not trouble him. From the point of view of a dog or animal, write a paragraph describing what you notice when you encounter Nathan and how you decide to proceed. Or, in the character of Mr. Murphy, write a secret BUM memo explaining how you will use this quality of Nathan's to help with spy efforts. Read your paragraphs and memos aloud to friends or classmates.

B. In chapter 14, Abigail quotes lines from Lewis Carroll's poem "The Walrus and the Carpenter" (*Through the Looking-Glass, and What Alice Found There*, 1871). Read the entire poem and, if possible, the dialogue that follows in the story. You may also choose to learn more about the poem, particularly the story of its illustration, and about Lewis Carroll's *Alice* books. Write a short essay explaining why you think David Lubar makes reference to this poem in his novel. Who (if anyone) do you think the Walrus and the Carpenter represent? Who might be the gullible oysters? What connections can you make between Carroll's work and the story of Nathan Abercrombie?

C. In order to help solve Nathan's undead problem, Mookie reads and watches every zombie book and movie he can find. Do you think this is a good way to help? If you were Nathan's friend, how might you help him try to find a solution to his problem? Write an outline of your plan to share with Nathan.

D. With friends or classmates, discuss whether Nathan would try the Hurt-Be-Gone and become a zombie if he had the chance to go back to that moment in time, and note the upsides and downsides of Nathan's zombie life. Then, individually, in the character of Nathan, write a speech beginning: "If I hadn't become a zombie, I never would have realized . . ."

QUESTIONS FOR DISCUSSION

1. As *The Big Stink* begins, why has Nathan's fifth-grade class been relocated to Borloff Lower Elementary? What physical features make this a challenge? Who else has been relocated to Borloff Lower? How does this affect lessons, lunchtime, and recess for Nathan and his friends? Compare this plan to the grade level organization of your school.

2. Mookie announces that the move to Borloff Lower "stinks." What other problems "stink," both literally and figuratively, in the course of the story?

3. Who are Rodney and Ridley Mullasco? What is Nathan's relationship to each of these boys? How would you describe the Mullascos' relationship to each other? Use quotes from the story to support your description. Do you think Rodney or Ridley is the worst bully? Explain your answer.

4. How does Nathan feel about being a spy for BUM? What is BUM's mission? Does this mission affect the way Nathan behaves in other

parts of his life? Give some examples to show how this might be the case.

5. Compare and contrast the different ways Abigail and Mookie try to help Nathan. Is one way better than the other? Do their strategies complement each other? Why or why not? Do you have friends who relate to you, and help you with problems, in different ways? Describe how this can be useful or challenging, using examples if possible.

6. What is "Bear Season," and how does Nathan's mom handle it? What is the result of her first attempt at costume ordering? Do you talk to your parents about their jobs? Do you know if they are relaxed or stressed about their work? Do you think parents should share information about their work with their kids? Why or why not?

7. Besides joining BUM, how has becoming a zombie changed Nathan's life? What physical changes have taken place and what is their result? How does Nathan deal with these changes? Why has Nathan begun to smell?

8. In chapter 9, Nathan says, "I thought about the cover of Mookie's comic book with all the badly rotted zombies. . . . I could hear the screams kids would make when they saw me. I'd be a real monster." How might you comfort Nathan at this moment in the story? What makes a "monster"? Do you agree with Dr. Cushing when she tells Nathan that "most adults would give up if they were in your situation. Don't ever think you lack courage" (chapter 13)? Explain.

9. How does Nathan feel about the various teachers and coaches who appear in the story? Do these teachers ever surprise him? Do you think he approaches his lessons with Mr. Murphy differently than his classroom lessons? Why or why not?

10. What skills does Nathan use when he sneaks aboard the garbage barge to intercept the RABID drop? Who comes to the rescue when the barge begins to sink? Who winds up rescuing whom? What realization does Nathan have while he is floating in the water?

11. In chapter 18, Nathan wishes he could use his zombie skills to help his mom with her troubles at Stuffy Wuffy. Is he able to do this and,

if so, how? What other problems does he solve at the same time? Does his being a zombie have anything to do with these other solutions? Why or why not?

12. Beyond an adventure about a rotting kid zombie, might *The Big Stink* be read as a story about seeing the connections between people, ideas, and situations? Who makes—or realizes how to make—such connections? What connections do you observe? Do you see any lessons in these connections that might apply to your own life?